Also by Cynthia Ozick

THE
CANNIBAL
GALAXY

THE
CANNIBAL
GALAXY

Cynthia
Ozick

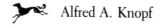 Alfred A. Knopf

New York   1983

THIS IS A BORZOI BOOK
PUBLISHED BY ALFRED A. KNOPF, INC.

Grateful acknowledgment is made to The Modern Library, a Division of
Random House, Inc., for permission to reprint an excerpt from
Aphrodite by Pierre Louÿs, translated by Lewis Galantiere. Copyright
1933 by The Modern Library, Inc.

Library of Congress Cataloging in Publication Data
Ozick, Cynthia. The cannibal galaxy.
  I. Title.
PS3565.Z5C3 1983   813'.54   82-48719
ISBN 0-394-52943-X

Manufactured in the United States of America
First Edition

for Bernard,
and for Rachel

The rest of Life to *see!*

Past Midnight! Past the Morning Star!

Emily Dickinson

Half the people love, half the people hate. And where is my place between these halves that are so well matched? And through what crack shall I see the white housing-projects of my dreams, and the bare-foot runners on the sands or, at least, the fluttering of the girl's kerchief, by the hill?

Yehuda Amichai

THE
CANNIBAL
GALAXY

The Principal of the Edmond Fleg Primary School was originally (in a manner of speaking) a Frenchman, Paris-born—but whenever he quoted his long-dead father and mother, he quoted them in Yiddish. "My son," he quoted his father, "when the teacher begins, *khapt men a dremele*. That's the time for a nap." The Principal had several such ancestral jokes, all at his own expense: he was a formidable elf. What was elfin was his twinkle, his grin, his sly fine teeth, the tricky downward slide of his eye, his ruddy shining skin. Behind all that he was a melancholic, a counter of losses. The children were not often afraid of him; the teachers were. Though he was Sorbonne-educated, his vowels strove to be American. Instead they palpitated with the unsuppressible inflections of the Rue des Rosiers. Since there were no Frenchmen in the neighborhood to catch him out, those vowels might once have flourished, for all any of the parents knew, in Bourbon throats.

The school was on a large lake in the breast-pocket of the continent, pouched and crouched in inwardness. It was as though it had a horror of coasts and margins; of edges and extremes of any sort. The school was of the middle and in the middle. Its three buildings were middling-high, flat-roofed, moderately modern. Behind them, the lake cast out glimmers of things primeval, cryptic, obscure. These waters had a history of turbulence: they had knocked freighters to pieces in tidal storms. Now and then the lake took human life.

In the mornings, well before the first rumble of the early buses, the Principal would come down from his dark and sagging rooms and run to the beach. He was a bachelor of fifty-eight, and still a good runner. In the misted green rain of May the water looked flat and impervious, as if a dead membrane had been stretched over it. The waves were without rise or fall. On other mornings the whole circle of the lake wheeled its dazzle of brass like another sun. Crayfish shells cut into the rubber of the Principal's sneakers. That was one side of the school.

The other side, where the buses parked, was hairy with unmown grass, jumbles of wild flowers, footpaths gone ragged. Hilly lawn followed tumbledown meadow, weed-frilled green splashed into the fuzz of dandelion puffs. After school, in the low light of afternoon (the school day was a long one), when the buses with their cargoes of bedlamites had departed, the Principal leaned into the ribs of these deserted fields; he leaned his breast toward the brown road, into the cup of the empty side field; at such moments, in the cut that came between the shrieks of two hundred children and the whited-out silence of the playground, he felt himself not so much a schoolmaster as a man of almost sacral power. He knew what lay in his hands: the miraculous ascent of lives, the future implicit in the present, the very goodness of humankind. *The world rests on the breath of the children in the schoolhouses*—this fragment of Talmud feathered his spirit like a frond from a tree in deep warmth.

On the beach side of the school, the lake side, he understood himself better. Shell shards and slimy rocks assaulted underfoot: nature's sheddings and bones. The track to the water a junkyard, the beach a trail of spotted junk. Here everything balanced: where

he had come from, where he had arrived. A lost shell. He thought
how even the stars are mere instances and artifacts of a topological
cartography of imagined dimensions; he reflected on that mathematical region wherein everything can be invented, and out of
which the-things-that-are select their forms of being from among
the illimitable plenitude of the-things-that-might-be.

He said to himself: *The Made and the Yet-to-Be-Made are equally
eloquent when expressed in their source-language, the divine locu-
tion of the equation; then who is to declare which is more comely,
which superior? What we deem to be Reality is only Partial Possibility coarsely ground into mere dumb Matter, a physicist's model
framed on the crude armature of gravity and chemicals.*

Gravity and chemicals! Atoms and forces! Crudity of systems.
The galaxies might easily be rough alternatives to some other
Principle yet untried in Matter. And the Principal himself—was
he too a rough alternative to some other man who might have
been standing there instead, on the cold sand?

Such meditations came to him less and less often as the years
drained. Nowadays his thought was rarely abstract. The abstract
stabbed—it was too personal. But he kept by him the bitter homo-
nym, the notion of Principle embodied in a Principal, his own
comfortless comical theory—ha!—of flawed incarnation. And he
held also to another secret pun, delivered by himself to himself
for the sole consequence of a nasty cackle: the Fleg of the Edmond
Fleg School, what is it short for? Answer: Phlegmatic. And what
else? Answer: Phlegethon, the river of fire that runs through Hell.

Though the school's lake was redolent of red men, forests,
Northern fogs, the Principal privately called it Lake Edmond
Phlegethon. Not that he imagined it aflame, even when a burning sunrise crumpled it crosswise; but he supposed the waters
boiled over a bed of old ash. He believed in the prevalence
of ash.

He saw himself in the middle of an ashen America, heading a
school of middling reputation (though he pretended it was better

than that), beleaguered by middling parents and their middling offspring. All of this was a surprise to his late middle age, but a surprise of only middling size. He was used to consorting with the Middle. He had been launched into the Middle of his time in every sense: close to the middle in a family of nine children, the fifth to wake alive in the cramped but broad-windowed flat above the Rue de Poitou, in the Marais, not far from his father's fish store in the very middle of the Rue des Rosiers—where, in the back room, among crates of fresh silvery mackerel and tall brown-glass bottles of brine, Rabbi Pult taught a class of five boys every evening, two of them Joseph's brothers Gabriel and Loup.

Joseph. The Principal's name was Joseph Brill. But he was known only as Principal Brill. Everyone said it just that way. Only the philanthropist who was the school's benefactress had ever dared to call him Joseph; all the rest, including all the parents and all the teachers, even the oldest, said Principal Brill. This title, with its syncopated engine, its locomotive rapidity, its tongue-twisting undercarriage, its lightfooted vibration, brought one to attention like an approaching express. The urgent stutter of its imperious syllables invested the air with civilization and authority.

Principal Brill scared and awed.

Τhe quickest way to go from home to his father's fish store was straight down the Rue Vieille du Temple, which led most directly to the Rue des Rosiers, with its teeming little shops, dim and odorous, and pavements dense with fruit hawkers and drygoods peddlers, vegetable carts and street criers, all in the dialects of the immigrants from Kiev and Minsk and Lithuania: a multitude drawn to the great capital and citadel of freedom: Paris the founder and purveyor of *fraternité* and *liberté*—catching up eighteen centuries late, Rabbi Pult said with a special pucker between his eyebrows, to the postulates and civilities of Hillel and Akiva. Joseph's job, after school, was to sweep and wash the wooden floors of the *poissonnerie*, sprinkle them with new sawdust, and then, when dusk began, hurry into the back room to straighten out the chairs in readiness for Rabbi Pult's arrival.

The walk down the Vieille du Temple pleased Joseph for one whole springtime: such a noble name, such reverence for the pieties and principles of an ancient people—a street called after the overrun and rubbled lost Temple of Jerusalem! He said this, or something like it, to his schoolmate Jean-Lucas, who hooted at him because he had never heard of Crusader knights. Jean-Lucas lent him a heap of books with pictures of castles, armor, horses, lances. And after that Joseph kept secret from his father and from Rabbi Pult everything he was savoring about damsels and dragons and chivalry and—he hardly let his eyes pluck at the words—the Holy Grail. They would have judged these enchanting and glorious histories to be frivolity, idolatry. Also from Jean-Lucas, whose uncle was a priest, Joseph picked up another bit of neighborhood lore: how, long ago, but only a few squares away, in the Cloître des Billettes, in the Rue des Archives, there had occurred the miracle of "Dieu Bouilli." A certain Jonathan le Juif, Jean-Lucas explained, having stolen the Host, the Body of God, boiled it and stabbed it; then the Host wept tears and cried for mercy in the Virgin's own voice. "That never happened really," Joseph said; the insult was preposterous; he had to hide his own profane tears. "Yes it did," Jean-Lucas insisted; "my uncle said so, and they punished all the Jews for it." So Joseph observed that—despite his father's immigrant gratitude for the privilege of *égalité*—he lived in a place where there had once been a pogrom no different from the pogrom in the savage Czarist village his parents had fled, and he avoided walking past the great gate of the Archives.

But there was another palace he liked to pass whenever he could, still without telling his father or Rabbi Pult. To get there, he had only to turn sharp left on the Vieille du Temple, into the Rue des Francs Bourgeois, and walk two streets over. It seemed to Joseph that this must be the loveliest house in the world. He stood under an archway and looked across a secret flowery courtyard emblazoned with statuary—how pleasant, how eerie, to think that real people had once slept in ordinary beds inside this delectable mansion! Stone wings enfolded the courtyard; stone masks laughed above the gateways—but Joseph did not recognize this sign of the carnival. Still, he was quick to intuit that he had come upon a singular elegance, though elegance itself was foreign to him. For one thing, venerable as the wondrous house was, he could tell it was not a church—not only because there were no crosses carved in the doors, but more particularly because he was not afraid. He would have been afraid of a church. The pure and shining doors stood alluringly open. Joseph peered into a darkling marvel—slowly wandering figures, like strolling dreamers, gazing at walls, colonnades, lions, mysterious stone ladies. Then he ran toward the *poissonnerie* in the Rue des Rosiers, and his broom.

He had a hidden name for this excursion: he called it "the roundabout way." And more and more he followed the roundabout way, tantalized by the beautiful house and its lordly contours. It was six months before he discovered what it was: the Musée Carnavalet. It was another six months before he found the courage to go in. And finally it was a year or so before it reached him that this had been the home of the astonishing Madame de Sévigné, though he did not yet understand who Madame de Sévigné was, or why she astonished.

The first time he dared to step into the Musée Carnavalet there were so many brilliant objects to seize his attention that he feared he would be late for the sweeping and the sawdust and the chairs if he lingered; so he churned past paintings and clocks and carved panels and golden plates and resplendent old costumes, determined to choose just one stone lady to stare at and moon over and remember. There she was, small, commanding, radiant, with a chin and mouth so perfectly bent on vitality that he waited for the lips to turn to rosy flesh and speak. Then he read a brass plaque and was stunned. The stone beauty was Rachel—who else if not Rachel the Mother of Israel, Rachel who weeps for her children as they pass before her on their way into their long Exile? It was only peculiar, in this Gentile homage, that the stone Rachel hardly looked pensive. If alive, she would break into hilarity.

That night, when Rabbi Pult had gone home (he lived around the corner, on the Rue des Ecouffes, over a kosher *boucherie*), Joseph confessed to his mother that he had been tempted to enter a large house, seemingly as public as any marketplace but with nothing for sale, where he had stumbled on a fine statue of Rachel the Matriarch. His mother instantly saw his trouble—she knew what a museum signified. A pagan hall had enticed him, an image had ensnared him. In such a place there would be throngs of sculptured unclothed women, an offense to modesty and a scandal of piety. "Save yourself from shame," she warned Joseph; "keep away from such a sty." "But it was Rachel the Mother of Israel," he protested. "An image is an image," she said, and he caught the burning of her eye.

He did keep away, at least for a while; his conscience was strong, and hummed with his mother's own inflections. But the round-about way was an ambush: it took him without his intending it, as if some immense magnet were pulling his very feet toward Number 23, Rue de Sévigné. The second time he went in, his heart knocked like a thief's. He felt like Jonathan le Juif—what sacred thing was he about to pinch, what arcane holiness not meant for him? He penetrated no farther than the first floor. Now he was inside Madame de Sévigné's own apartment. Her bed stood just as it had three centuries earlier. He knew himself to be a violator of these curious scrolls and moldings, of these alien mirrors, of that great bed. A wide corridor preceded her salon. He moved deeper into the strangeness, and came face to face with Madame de Sévigné herself: his mother had been nearly right—she was almost completely nude, down to the very top of her bosom, where the lace frill made a pretty border. Pearls were sewn into the voluptuous sleeves of her gown—ah, these had the shapes of crosses at last. Her stout neck was encircled by a wreath of very fat pearls—they resembled little turnips—and, though her head was somewhat turned from him, still another fat pearl glinted at the one ear that peeped out. Her hair, with its ghostly veil trailing behind, was all ringlets, her eyebrows were smooth and shapely, her nose was unrefined (a bit too spare at the bridge, a bit too coarse at the tip), her jawline disappeared into the plumpness of the too-thick neck, even her wrists were not slender enough—but the lips and eyes were vessels of wit; the small curled mouth had just swallowed a *bon mot,* and shone with appetite for more. The longer Joseph took in this portrait, the more inexplicably at ease he grew in those rooms, despite all their awesome silver and gold. Not far from Madame de Sévigné was another painting that seemed to be paired with the first: it was of a younger woman, haughtier, cooler, much more beautiful: the brass plaque announced that this was the Comtesse de Grignan, the daughter of Madame de Sévigné.

It was not until years later, when Joseph had already crossed the Seine to the Sorbonne, that he learned who these antique yet lively women were. The mother, according to one source, was "insane"—she loved her daughter obsessively, pathologically, so much so that she spent her life penning her longing in letter after letter. "How I should like to have a letter from you! It is nearly half an hour since I received the last!" she once wrote. This did not make Joseph laugh. He was by now too ardently a Frenchman. Frenchmen might be amused, but never by the brocaded weight of the literature of France—and (who could believe such a surprise?) Madame de Sévigné had molded the literature of France. "From Carnavalet," Joseph read, "came the purest and most perfect French hitherto written in the land." From his own roundabout way! Madame de Sévigné's unreasonable passion for her undistinguished daughter had turned the mother's prose into high culture and historic treasure. Joseph did not tell this to Rabbi Pult, and certainly not to his hardworking parents, still scraping scales and lifting out fish skeletons to make the clean white filets that lay on shaved ice in snowy rows, all for the sake of his drinking in Western Civilization at the University. He was a serious student, and felt it his obligation to keep it from his parents that Western Civilization was sometimes not serious. It seemed natural to them that he was immersed in Latin—ancient languages are always serious—but what would they have thought of Catullus? *Let's live and love, my Lesbia. . . . Give me a thousand kisses, and then a hundred, and then another thousand. . . .* Catullus and Madame de Sévigné were separated by an aeon, but what good friends they were! Joseph still did not laugh—in fact, it hurt and shamed him—when he remembered the guilty blunder of his boyhood: how, at his first visit to the Musée Carnavalet, he had mistaken the effigy of an actress, famous for her red slippers and for her strenuous arms and voice transported upward, for the biblical Rachel. The theatrical Rachel, the Rachel of *Phèdre*, it was true, had been a Jewish woman; and it was a marvel that the lovers Héloïse and Abélard were buried in a mausoleum in the Jewish Cemetery, and that Anatole France, with his stirring surname, could also have been a Jew. France—Paris especially—could allow and even embrace such curiosities and accidents, but curiosities and accidents were not France. France knew what it was, and Joseph, nibbling his roll brought from home at a café table with his book propped against a coffee cup, knew too. He no longer made such blunders. He was in command of his neighborhood—not its hawkers and stalls, but the secrets of the old Paris. Diagonally across the street from the Carnavalet, in tiny lodgings, in a corner of a mansion once inhabited by the illegitimate daughter of Henri II, Daudet had received Turgenev, Zola, Flaubert. Some steps farther, in the Place des Vosges, in a seventeenth-century house of red brick, Victor Hugo had bent over the manuscript of *Les Misérables*: a few doors down, Rachel had powdered her white face—the red-slippered actress, not the Mother of Israel. Richelieu had occupied Number 21. It was an easy trot, winding down from the fish store on the Rue des Rosiers along the Rue St. Antoine to the Bastille: the very spot where modernity began.

The University inspired him to alter his diction—fumy, Joseph discovered, with the odors of the shops on the Rue des Rosiers. His friends, new ones from *arrondissements* to the west and north, did not sound their vowels as he did; it was humiliating to be an immigrant's child and fill one's mouth with the wrong noise. Every night Joseph scrubbed the fish smell off his hands with an abrasive soap that skinned his knuckles mercilessly.

He studied literature for a while—the nuances of Verlaine maddened him with idolatrous joy; he was swimming in Gide and Montherlant—but then found, because of the joy, that he could not justify it. He was ashamed, before his parents, always to be reading ecstatically, uselessly. His father was more sympathetic than his mother; he had sometimes heard his father remark on the iridescence of the scales of the ordinary *morue*, how a fish could become a mosaic of rainbows. His father perhaps did not altogether despise poetry and novels. But both his father and his mother looked into his books anxiously—what was this, what did that mean, and how could one get one's living from such trivia? "*Futilité*," his mother said. "*Narishkayt*," his father said—but not without a certain sad gesture of his scraping-knife.

"Your family wishes your interests were more cosmic," his new friend Claude mocked; Claude's father was the director of an automobile company, in which certain ornate old great-aunts held shares. Sometimes in the mornings Claude would lead Joseph to the Louvre—a magnificence Joseph had never before entered— and point out the darker paintings and sermonize on them; Claude was an aesthete. But he was also a pragmatist: he knew which were all the right cafés, and he knew what subjects one would naturally exclude from elevated talk, and which lecturers to avoid as being almighty bores. Claude got himself and Joseph invited to dinner with old Borys Korzeniowski-Conrad, the novelist's elder son, who had come from England to visit with Polish relations in the Rue Caulaincourt. Joseph's English was far from fluent, and Korzeniowski-Conrad's French sounded exactly like English—later Claude explained that old Borys had spoken at length of his father's irritability and lonely scowl. For all Joseph had understood, old Borys had said only that the soup was too much salted; all the other guests instantly agreed. Joseph himself did not taste the soup, or anything else. He chewed anxiously on a bit of bread. Another time Claude told Joseph that it might be a lark to visit a certain old writer who lived in London, and that if Joseph would consent to go, Claude would foot the bill for the two of them. Joseph's parents thought it a wild expedition with no sane purpose, to cross the Channel to England only to sit on a hard chair while an Englishman read from an unpublished manuscript in an incomprehensible barbarian tongue; and his mother became even angrier when she learned that Claude would pay for everything. "You will be indebted," she admonished Joseph. "No," Joseph said, "he insists I mustn't ever pay him back; he says it's all right." "Then you will be still more indebted." They argued for days, but in the end he went.

The Channel was so choppy that Claude was reluctant to venture out on deck, and made Joseph stay with him below, reading. For his birthday Claude had given Joseph an English translation of Pierre Louÿs's *Aphrodite*. "Now you can practice your neander-thal English and relinquish your stupid Israelite squeamishness all at the same time!" Claude himself had recently become an enthusiast of Paul Valéry, and was browsing in a chapter of *Variété*. "Listen to this bit," Claude, curled in his bunk, called to Joseph. Joseph came and stood near Claude's bed, looking down into Claude's book. "This is how he describes Leonardo's naked sketches:

Here and there he has drawn anatomical unions, horrible cross-sections of love itself. He is fascinated by the erotic machine, the mechanics of living bodies being his favorite domain. Horrible cross-sections, Joseph! The erotic machine, Joseph!" The cabin tilted, catapulting Valéry out of Claude's grasp, and *Aphrodite* out of Joseph's, and jolting Joseph first toward the low ceiling, and then more or less into Claude's arms; it seemed the two of them were confined inside some vast tossing cradle. Joseph was uneasy; was Claude embracing him from behind, or was he, like a good fellow, preventing him from breaking his neck? He began to feel a mystery about Claude, into whose peculiarly welcoming bed, during the cabin's last frantic seizure, he had been thrown, or had fallen, or had perhaps been purposefully drawn.

In the snug little sitting room in London with its out-of-season gas fire where the grate ought to have been, Claude appeared to be acquainted not only with the old writer—whose feathery mustache and round back presented him as a somewhat diffident yet dignified brown grouse—but with a surprising number of the other listeners in the room. It struck Joseph that there were no women, and that some of the young men were holding each other's hands. "It's from a book he will never publish in his lifetime," Claude whispered; then he took Joseph's hand. This made Joseph proud: he admired Claude, his accent, his haughty old great-aunts, his curiosity about sensuality, his worship of beautiful things and beautiful words, his quickness with foreign tongues. The diffident yet dignified brown grouse was reciting out loud:

He saw their small faces: vessels of purity. Their faces would never be pulled about like an old string-bag. A republic apart, his pupils, pupils of his heart, pupils of his eyes. He saw by means of their pure round limbs. They were his trees: branches and moist twigs. The exquisite rows of his lads put him in mind of those Japanese horticulturists who cultivate great oaks by dwarfing them in hand-sized pots. Like these fond gardeners, he knew what it was to cherish the delectably stunted. His pygmy men: they would always be miniature, they would never rise to shake their leafy heads high in the arbor. They were his own blessed and chosen nation, his pygmy republic. They would not marry. He had never known the death of any of them. They would never touch women or corpses. They would rarely touch grief. They would never bear fruit. They would be fair-faced and beardless into eternity.

It was an elegantly-voweled passage meticulously read, the casting of Joseph's own life. Quizzically, very kindly, the old writer asked to be introduced to Joseph. Joseph protested that his English was not good enough, that he had not comprehended three-quarters of the story. "You're a Hebrew lad, isn't that so?" the old writer said. Joseph said he was. "That's all right, then. You're on the side of Demeter, though you deny her. You'll be a teacher. You'll marry. Claude," the old writer said, pulling his fingers—how tender they were!—through Joseph's black hair, "this young David will marry, remember that."

"Your London hero thinks he's an oracle," Joseph complained to Claude on the boat-train going home. "I don't want anything to do with teaching." But Claude was glum. He had turned private, taciturn. The crossing to Calais was far calmer. They stood together on the dock, pushing into the straight and steady wind, and Joseph knew before it happened that Claude would kiss him, and in a special way, not as two bold friends kiss. Joseph had in fact never kissed anyone other than his father and mother and his sisters and brothers. He was unsure whether he liked it; it frightened him terribly; it made him think of Leviticus.

After that he kept away from Claude. Claude was scornful, and called him Dreyfus, and inveigled his friends into calling him Dreyfus too. Joseph was again isolated; it was, he discovered, more difficult for him to find intellectual heroes than it had ever been for Claude. Even Voltaire could not be trusted; even Voltaire had contempt for Leviticus. Reluctantly, Joseph brought this news to Rabbi Pult. Rabbi Pult was not astounded. "What is the Enlightenment?" Rabbi Pult said. "Joseph, the Enlightenment engendered a new slogan: There is no God, and the Jews killed him. Joseph, this is the legacy of your Enlightenment." So Joseph abandoned literature and history, the side of the mind that, whatever pictures and illuminations might be hung there, was like a cave teeming with bestial forms; he looked for a place without a taint. He thought beyond the planet; he thought of the stars. His parents were pleased when they understood Joseph was going to study "the most universal thing of all"—they assumed he meant medicine, healing, reversing injury and pain. But he meant just the opposite: remoteness. He was sick of human adventure. He had felt an unknowable warmth and feared it. It had betrayed him and named him Dreyfus. He matriculated under the formidable Georges Gaillard, the discoverer of Gaillard's Teapot—*La Théière du Gaillard*—and set out to learn the cold, cold skies.

The lake—or so it seemed to Joseph Brill when he first stared out into its smoky gray infinitude—was the size of the Mediterranean. Remarkably, it had the sandy shore of a sea. The sand and the waves—saltless waves, curly and true—surprised him: astronomer or no, it had not occurred to him that the water of the heartland, inner water, so to speak—middle water—would also be moon-drawn, licking and tumbling and cresting into white rooster-combs, exactly like the planet's more exogenous waters. The lake was an inside ocean: birds screeched into its blue, shells stuck up like toenails in its strand. It might even have harbored a swimming dragon.

Human habitation framed the lake (though unseen: Joseph Brill could descry only the arching shore on one side, no more than that; the rest of the frame had to be taken on faith), and in this, too, it was like the Mediterranean, Europe's old puddle. But Europe's old puddle lapped at the isles of Greece, and at Italy's wrinkly boot-snout, and at Jaffa, that regretful port-town Jonah's ship left behind, and, especially, at the hot mellow underskirt of France, the carnival city of Nice. Wherever Europe's old puddle touched, it touched history, antiquity, happening. Here nothing had happened.

So the school was high and dry, left out to age in the middle of America—"the middle of America" being the very phrase that often came to Principal Brill at Commencement time, when he had to formulate his speech: this middleness, it privately smote him, was the cause of the mediocrity, or worse, of the school's architecture. The Edmond Fleg Primary School had the forthright design of a freight train on the move: three hapless boxcars. The first, "the old section," was of red-brick construction; the last two, having earned the higher grace of "the new wing," were built of great dark cinderblocks. All three were lined up in a row as if bound for a destination, though there was nowhere to go but a wilderness of meadows. So innocently American was the architect of the new wing that he had not dreamed, Joseph Brill was certain, of boxcars; but boxcars rolling eastward had taken away Joseph Brill's mother, father, his brothers Gabriel and Loup, his little sisters Michelle and Louise (who had altered her name, all on her own, from Leah), his baby sister Ruth, and released their souls into an ash field. Now and then he encountered newspaper photos of that expanse of human meal: flowers grew richly from it, stirring their brilliant caps. It was easy for him, when he saw the straight march of his school, the old section taller and wider and brighter than the new wing, and the new wing following in its narrow dark doubleness, to think of boxcars.

The old section had once been a furniture factory—but exclusively for the manufacture of chairs—owned by a family called

Bristol. Sunk in the sand were remains of an ancient dock, where tugboats drawing the long cargo barges used to anchor—barges carrying crated chairs as far north as Port Arthur, as far south as New Orleans, and then by train all over North America. Chairs of every shape and kind had come into being in these uniform rooms, under windows high but stiflingly slender, like rectangular portholes through which sky and lake could flash—no single type was more popular than the Bristol chair itself. A model Bristol, one of particular nobility (it was the globe version, minus its cross), stood in the Principal's office, behind the Principal's own desk; carved out of glowing cherrywood, it had eight back spindles (this aspect gave it a slight resemblance to the Windsor chair), the usual four legs, though slanted outward (again like the Windsor), but only one arm, which ended almost shockingly in the replica of a wooden hand. The hand was rendered with a charming faithfulness, elevating the whole into a sort of sculpture: but it was what the hand was made to hold that especially distinguished the Bristol chair in its prime. Often the hand gripped a runner's torch, into which an electric bulb (when such things were newfangled) could be inserted. Other versions supplied the hand with a wooden bowl of artificial fruit, including a glass apple turned golden by the insertion of an electric bulb; or a painted glass globe of the world, illuminated by electric bulb from within, a wooden cross triumphantly on top.

But all that was long ago. When Joseph Brill came to it, the old section was an abandoned factory building a few yards from an abandoned stable that had once been attached to an abandoned farmhouse. There was no farmhouse even then: a wand of light-ning blazing out of the lake had set it afire; nearby, the stark masts of charred pickets were all that was left of a grove of tulip trees. Out of this ruin, half brick, half black, drowned in green, the Edmond Fleg Primary School rose.

It rose partly because of the ambitiousness of a rich benefactress, and partly on a theory. The theory was Joseph Brill's. It was not a new theory—in the history of the Jews no theory is—and it was the kind of theory that usually begins in music: Bach, for instance, from whom no human heart wishes to be excluded. But for Joseph Brill an early strand of the theory had unraveled itself in a schoolhouse (not this one), in the middle of the war, when his mother and father and brothers Gabriel and Loup and little sisters Michelle, Louise, and Ruth had already been taken away. He did not know what had become of his three older sisters—the ABCs, he used to call them: Anne, Berthe, Claire. They were energetic and resourceful girls. He himself (but it was a long story, and he did not often tell it) had been hidden for a time by four nuns in a storage room in the subcellar of a convent school. The nuns were themselves theorists of a sort; for one thing, they were vegetarians. Their speech was so old-fashioned as to be nearly archaic. His only companions in the cellar were numerous mice and the books heaped on low platforms to save them from the damp floor. He read whatever was there. The four conspirator-nuns who had concealed him believed, with God's help, he would end by turning Christian; they fed him what they could, and left his mind to feed itself. Among themselves they referred to him as *l'astronome*, and apologized to him for imprisoning him out of sight of the stars. He apologized for the pail of excrement they daily carried away. When he was ill—this happened frequently, because of the dampness, and then the pail had to be carried away much more often—they could not bring him a doctor, but put down a thermos of broth to "get him through the night," as if, in his perpetual blackness, they expected him to know night from day. In his secret thoughts he named his place and his plight *nox perpetua*, and kept his little lamp burning even while he slept. The darkness was like a doom, and terrible, and permanent, though one day he would long for it. He read like a maniac. In the main the books were worn-out school texts and catechisms; he did not care what he read. But after a stretch of this—time was amorphous—his four saviors lugged down to him a huge and enticing library, all in what seemed no more than a week or so, straining down the unlit stone stairs under the troubled weight of box after cumbrous box, until he found his cot surrounded by a maze of boxes, each loaded tight with books, but without order of any kind. An old priest, a virtuoso friend of the convent (his sisters had been educated there), had died not long before. The nuns were proud of him—an intellectual, more than a simple holy man, though he had been that as well—and were gratified to have been given interim charge of his spiritual possessions. His library was too remarkable; it was not conventional. The Bishop had requested them to sort and catalogue at their leisure. They understood this meant the Bishop wished them to relieve him of the old priest's baggage: he had had a dangerous reputation for liberalism. The old priest's baggage saved Joseph Brill's sanity; so he speculated years afterward.

"I lost my mind," he would describe it, "but I didn't go mad. I only acquired someone else's mind for a while." The old priest had read (this was a surprise) novels and plays. Inside a stately dark-green leather-bound volume of Corneille, Joseph discovered a mysterious poem composed in a violent hand, in two languages, by (he assumed) the virtuoso priest himself:

> Mon âme de serre grossit
> comme une grenade d'hiver
> qui va éclater.
> Rupture de semence
> tourbillone le clair ruisseau.
> Comme le cerf abbatu dans le veld

le ruisseau rouge saigne
pour contenter ma soif.

My hothouse soul is swelled
like a winter pomegranate
about to burst.
Rupture of seeds
swirls the clear brook.
Like the hart shot in the veld
the red brook bleeds
to please my thirst.

Did this signify religion, or love, or some other turmoil? There
were stacks of poetry volumes—Joseph had gratefully volunteered
to sort—and much philosophy and theology. Gradually it came
clear to him that the old priest had loved thought more than Jesus;
Jesus was one of his thoughts; he had not always been in a state of
full faith. One day (or more likely it was night, since no one was
bringing him a meal) Joseph dug out a strange book. He could
not tell whether it was Jewish or Christian. The name of it was
Jésus, raconté par le Juif Errant, by one Edmond Fleg; out fell a
fragile bit of paper, again in the priest's old-fashioned stormy
alphabet, with a quotation from Heinrich Heine: *The lizards on a
certain hillside have reported that the stones expect God to mani-
fest Himself among them in the form of a stone.* What mockery!
And who was Edmond Fleg? Joseph splashed his hands (how sore
they had become in the dungeon that was his haven, the knuckles
often bleeding) through volume after volume, coughing with
impatience: what else had Edmond Fleg set down? Was he a
Christian or a Jew? To which world did he belong? Eventually
Joseph turned up four or five volumes of plays: the title that drew
him was *Le Juif du Pape*. He read it in a gulp: it was about an
encounter between Pope Clement VII and Solomon Molcho, the
Marrano visionary burned by the Inquisition. Then he happened
on a lyrical little book, which seemed autobiographical, called

L'Enfant prophété: Fleg's metaphysical travels, he saw, led from
agnosticism to Hebrew sympathies, but via a Jewish Jesus. He
liked better Fleg's translation into French of *Julius Caesar.* There
was more. The old priest had been a collector, an admirer, of
Edmond Fleg. In the margins of *Pourquois je suis Juif* there was
still another sample of the old priest's hand and thought:

> The Israelitish divinely unifying impulse and the Israelitish ethical
> inspiration are the foundations of our French genius. Edmond Fleg
> brings together all his visions and sacrifices none. He harmonizes
> the rosette of the Légion d'Honneur in his lapel with the frontlets
> of the Covenant on his brow.

Similar notes tracked through the pages of *Ecoute Israël,* which
seemed to be a kind of verse cycle, and of a long essay, *Ma
Palestine.* In a decade or so Edmond Fleg, *né* Flegenheimer, had
gone from skeptical playwright and (Joseph imagined) stylish Parisian boulevardier to a Jew panting for Jerusalem. The old priest
had often tarried inside Edmond Fleg's mind. Joseph brooded on
Rabbi Pult.

They had taken him away the very morning after Joseph had
stayed the night in Rabbi Pult's flat on the Rue des Ecouffes,
helping Rabbi Pult pack his books. Rabbi Pult, unlike Joseph's
parents, was preparing for a journey. As a farewell present he gave
Joseph his old creased briefcase, with a treasure inside: the treatise
Ta'anit, an ancient copy printed in Venice, received by Rabbi
Pult's own teacher, and now passed on to Joseph to link teacher
with pupil, a linking meant to be carried forward into the horizons
of the farthest future—"You, will be a teacher," he announced to
Joseph, exactly as the old writer in London had. But Joseph was
already on his own line; he was well into his advanced degree and
had been assisting Gaillard in the observatory until Gaillard
suggested it was perhaps, for the time being, better not to. Despite
his intimacy with the galaxies—"the orbs are human levelers, not

political levers" was his catchphrase; he said this in English, for the play on "level" and "lever"—Gaillard had become narrowly uneasy about his Jewish students. He had a brother-in-law in a high ministry at Vichy. Joseph felt how naïve Rabbi Pult was about the future altogether—as if, in such a Europe, there could now be a future at all. They went on packing in silence, filling suitcases. Rabbi Pult's library was sparser than the old priest's, more condensed, less distracted; it was hardly a banquet; it had a certain austere concentration. It was like a dipper of ocean water: all the elements that are in the ocean are in the dipper. There was, moreover, not a single volume in French. For Rabbi Pult the future remained as clarified as it had ever been: it was the white space into which messianic redemption would intervene. Joseph sometimes pretended to himself a conversation between Gaillard and Rabbi Pult, on the subject of the heavens. How unschooled each would think the other! It embittered Joseph to know that the work at the observatory went on very well without him.

In the morning Rabbi Pult sent him home. Something was happening: all the streets radiating out from the Rue des Rosiers were distraught, overrun with police. It was still too early for his father to have opened the *poissonnerie*; he should warn his father to stay away from this commotion. As he neared his own house on the Rue de Poitou—he was running like a madman—the shouts and the roil began to subside. The stairwell was quiet, almost sleepy. He raced up three flights and found everything tranquil, everything in its place—the bread on the table, half sliced, the knife lying mutely on a white dish. Everyone was gone. The summer heat shimmered at the open window. He flew back to the Rue des Ecouffes, Rabbi Pult's old briefcase with the *Ta'anit* in it numbing his fist; he did not understand what he was doing, or why. In the twenty minutes between his leaving the Rue des Ecouffes and his return, fire and steam had transformed the world: the glass of the *boucherie* below Rabbi Pult's flat was smashed. It became more and more urgent to cry out that his family had disappeared (but he did not understand what he was doing, or why); when he came to Rabbi Pult's door, it was torn off its upper hinge, hanging crazily; no one was there. In the middle of the floor he saw all the books they had packed into suitcases the night before, dumped out. Some were burned to ash, some only charred. The invaders had made a bonfire, enjoyed it for a time, then doused it. A puddle still trickled from the center of the pyre; a transparent spiral of vapor curled out of its flank. The dead books reeked of ruin, flame, animal hides, a fetid steaminess. in the streets creatures like centaurs scuttled and scrabbled, flinging their rods, sticks, rocks, poles. Metamorphosis and shock. Fangs, hoofs, strange hairinesses. Uniforms everywhere. Noble French youth. Gendarmes, patrolmen, baby-faced students from the police school, hundreds of cross-strapped blue shirts and armbands. The gutters of Paris a wilderness. Sweat spilled from behind Joseph's ears down into the well of his collarbone; it was July. He hurtled himself back toward home for some clothes to take with him; then grew suddenly sane: it was folly to go back. Instead he ran, he ran nowhere; he ran. There were mobs moving toward the Seine and its bridges; he veered, and ran the other way. His throat roared with a burning; his ribs were in agony. He discovered that he was praying for his three older sisters—only what seemed to be prayer of the lung was merely panting and throat-pain. In his new sanity he admonished himself to come to a halt. His legs would not obey. Then he ordered them to show dignity, fearlessness, to slacken, to stroll, to saunter, to walk. At a cruelly casual pace, the blood gyrating in his neck, he wandered through Paris, himself its prey, reminding his numb fist that it was more unobtrusive to swing than to clutch Rabbi Pult's briefcase containing the Venetian *Ta'anit*. He swung the *Ta'anit* upward—mother! With the next mercilessly slow step, downward—father! Brothers! Sisters! He was running again. The ABCs had deserted the flat on the Rue de Poitou a month before, and had gone to work in separate factories; they had talked of getting away to Sweden, or even

England. Rabbi Pult, by contrast, spoke only of "taking a trip." Joseph, panting and praying, his throat bloated, tried to visualize the neat little settlement-towns in Poland his parents and brothers and little sisters were being led to: perhaps Ruth, who was only two, would forget all her French, and would have to grow up speaking Polish. But he was too sane to believe any of this. Nevertheless he did not dream where his family, at that very instant, might actually be: no more than half a mile distant, having been herded and driven with nine thousand others into the Vélodrome d'Hiver, a sports stadium in the fifteenth *arrondissement* whose ramparts he had glimpsed only half an hour ago, reflecting the morning's honeyed sunlight. He was too many streets away by now to be among those good citizens who could hear the moaning, soughing, and sobbing behind the Vél d'Hiv's walls as the day's heat gathered. He did not know that his mother and father, Gabriel and Loup, Michelle, Louise, and Ruth would live for a week penned up in that spot without food or toilets, in the open, body jammed into body, under a devouring sun, squatting or sprawling among the faint and the dying, day after day, the bawling of the infants rising, never lessening, until the terrifying and delusive relief of the coming of the trucks—and then the loading and unloading, the brutal hiatus in Drancy, and again the loading into boxcars, and again the unloading, the undressing, the run to the false showers. In Poland.

All that day and the days afterward, while Joseph was sauntering over the face of Paris, sauntering and swinging the Venetian *Ta'anit*, then exploding into a run, then again swinging and sauntering, his baby sister Ruth, in the Vél d'Hiv, screamed and screamed; but he did not know or hear. He made himself think of her growing up without the clear murmur of French in her mouth, in Poland; he made himself think of the ABCs in Sweden, in England; he made himself think of Rabbi Pult; he made himself think of Joseph Brill, a fugitive, temporarily fallen into a hole in the grid of roundup and capture, caught. Dead.

He was not caught; his life was a miracle, he was miraculously at leisure in a dungeon, wallowing in the old priest's massive library. It *was* a wallow, this endless resting, this endless reading, this endless Fleg, this endless indulgence of being alive and not caught. For a day or so he switched to St. Augustine. He tried a bit of Rousseau. He seldom looked into Rabbi Pult's *Ta'anit*—he did not like to open its sweet letters into such a smell. It was a cellar-smell; it was the smell of his jail and his pail. But also it seemed to him sometimes that the nuns, when they came with his supper of bread and cheese and their smiles, carried the odor of candles in their habits: a continual burning, a smokiness. The pyre. He could not breathe when they were near. They fetched away his pail to empty it; they gave him food and their steady smiles, as steady as if they were screaming without stopping—but of course they were immensely hushed, and he guessed that in the normal world of upstairs daylight they were nearly as still. Silence was in their dress and gait. Almost never did they tell him of a danger, a close call, a relief, but he smelled it in their smiles. He did not know how they managed his concealment.

They brought him a radio; he could listen, if he liked, to the war. There was only one electrical outlet: it was either the lamp or the radio. In the blackness he heard the ranting against the Jews and preferred the lamp—he had grown intimate with the old priest's nomad intellect, and sank into it again when his tending nun went away. He whispered his thanks in her wake. He thanked his nuns each time for each moment: each moment was his life. To hide the radio's vulgar brown face (the knobs like cruel eyes), he laid the *Ta'anit* on top of it. Then he noticed that the *Ta'anit*, also leather-bound, also dark green, almost exactly matched the old priest's volume of Corneille—at first sight you could not tell the difference. They were nearly a pair.

In that instant he was shot through by his idea. If they did not hunt him out, if he lived, if the war ended and he survived it, he would fulfill Rabbi Pult's exhortation and the old writer's prediction: he would be a teacher, and marry, and unite his two minds.

He understood he had two. In this he was like Edmond Fleg. *He brings together all his visions and sacrifices none.*

So it came to Joseph Brill, imprisoned in a school, that he would found a school. It was a thought infinitely remote, mazy and tantalizing—a school run according to the principle of twin nobilities, twin antiquities. The fusion of scholarly Europe and burnished Jerusalem. The grace of Madame de Sévigné's flowery courtyard mated to the perfect serenity of a purified Sabbath. Corneille and Racine set beside Jonah and Koheleth. The combinations wheeled in his brain. He saw the civilization that invented the telescope side by side with the civilization that invented conscience—astronomers and God-praisers uniting in a majestic dream of peace.

Then and there he contrived a solitary game:

He opened the *Ta'anit* and read to himself in a smothered theatrical hoarseness:

Rav happened to come to a certain place where there was no rain. He ordered a fast, but the rain did not come. Then the reader of the congregation went down to the praying desk and recited "He causes the wind to blow," and immediately a wind blew, and when he recited "He causes the rain to fall," rain fell. Rav therefore asked him: "What is thy occupation?" "I am a teacher of young children," the reader replied, "and I teach the children of the poor as well as those of the rich, and if anyone is so poor that he is unable to pay, I take no fee from him. I possess a fish pond, and if a child is careless in his studies, I bribe him by giving him some of the fish and thus win him over to study."

Pult, Pult! Pult of the pyre! Whom he had taught nothing but the joke of the Enlightenment! Pult who kept school among fish!

Then he reached at random into one of the old priest's boxes and drew out whatever his hand fell on. It was Proust: *Sodome et Gomorrhe.* He opened it and read, in the same kind of suppressed growl:

By a transposition of the senses, M. de Cambremer looked at you
with his nose. This nose of his was not ugly, it was if anything too
handsome, too bold, too proud of its own importance. Arched,
polished, gleaming, brand new, it was amply prepared to atone for
the inadequacy of his eyes. Unfortunately, if the eyes are sometimes
the organ through which our intelligence is revealed, the nose (to
leave out of account the intimate solidarity and the unsuspected
repercussion of one feature upon the rest), the nose is generally the
organ in which stupidity is most readily displayed.

The juxtaposition made him laugh. A joke, a joke! He had
never before laughed down here; there was a minute stir, a muffled
rustle, as if someone else was present, lurking and watching. He
gave half a shudder and half a jump. He knew he was alone, and
in this clarified aloneness he drank up the terrific truth of both
passages, the Aramaic and the French, each chosen, as in a
lottery, by an idle riffle. Rav and Proust, the half-Jew (on his
mother's side; hence, according to the Jewish code, as much a Jew
as Rav himself), both measured the world, one by passion for the
ideal, the other by passion for the sardonic detail. How different
they were! *And neither told a lie.* This was a marvel, that two
souls, two such separated tonalities, so to speak, could between
them describe the true map of life.

—There *was* someone else. Someone was sitting on the bottom
stair, lurking and watching. In a plenitude of grief he took it in
that it was all over for him. He was vomitous with regret—what
had he done wrong, what mistake, misstep, disloyalty, discord-
ance? How had he failed his nuns, or they him? The watcher
moved toward him, a little thing. He seized the radio, held it over
his head, and prepared to hurl it: he hoped the tubes would
implode and a bit of glass lodge in the little thing's eyes. Then he
heard the little thing's voice: "Etes-vous l'Abbé Martin?" He swallowed down a full mouth of nausea—he felt he was frothing, like
a rabid dog—and said yes. "Soeur Thérèse warned us there could

be an inspection at any time, there might be a stranger at any time, in any corner of the school, even a surprising place, and it would be you." The nuns had never told him this. "Why did you come down here?" he said. "Because of the Jews." Again he gripped the radio—what kind of charade could it be? "When they are angry they call me Jew." "Who calls you Jew?" "My best friends. Françoise. Germaine." "Isn't that dangerous? Why do you stand for it? Come into the light." She sat down on his cot under the lamp; immediately he was ashamed that it was not neat, littered with his wild blanket and a dozen or so of the old priest's books. He was looking at a girl of fifteen, hazel-eyed behind spectacles, curly-haired, wearing the convent uniform, altogether plain. Nevertheless he was afraid. She had clever nostrils. "Why did you come down here?" he said again; "you know the sisters don't allow it." "To cool off. Otherwise I would kill them. I have the temper of a murderer when they begin. I've been here before. I've seen you before. It's interesting to watch a priest make pee-pee like just anybody. Once I saw you make pee-pee into the pail."

He wondered what he ought to do. He could not bash her temples with the radio, or strangle her; even if he could, and if he pressed her carcass into one of the big book boxes, what would be the good of it? It would decay; it would smell; he would be found out. Upstairs they would miss the girl. The nuns would not keep on a man who had killed. Finished; he was finished. "They made me change my name," the girl said. "What is your name?" "Renée." "What's the matter with Renée?" Great God, to be having such a conversation in such a place, with the noose already around his neck! "Levin. They made it Le Fèvre. But I don't care who knows. Everyone knows." "You're a Jew," he said; but felt no relief. More than ever he wanted to annihilate her voice; he wanted to pulverize her for being there. "I'm a Catholic," she said; "the third generation in our family. My grandfather on my father's side was the first. The sisters say I'm a blood relative of

Our Lord." "But you're a Jew." "I don't care. I'm not afraid." He said, "You make me afraid for you." This was deceitful. He was afraid for himself. "You shouldn't be so open," he said; "you'll endanger everyone around you." "Everyone knows anyhow. All the girls know." "You'll endanger the sisters." "All the sisters know." "Where are your parents?" "They went away with my aunt and made me stay here." Now he did not know what he should say. "Renée," he said, "you shouldn't spy like this. Don't come back." "I'm not normal. They gave me a psychological test." He wanted to send her away, but he was afraid; every strange sentence she spoke frightened him more. "Go and get Soeur Thérèse," he said. "She'll punish me for sneaking down here." "How? How will she punish you?" "She'll make me copy out half of *Julius Caesar*, in English." A flash of Fleg; he felt he would laugh again. He was helpless. He wanted to vomit and he wanted to laugh; he was a dead man. He said instead: "Good. It will improve your English and your scholarship." "What do you do here all the time?" "It's my job. I'm being punished too. I disobeyed the Bishop and he sent me down here to catalogue a deceased priest's library." "Do you hate it?" "Yes," he said, "I hate it."

After that he kept his eye perpetually on the staircase; he discovered that he had an ineradicable and incessant tremor. Also he had a burning sensation when he urinated; he was miserable from it. He could not tell whether it was the urine that burned, or the bottom of his spleen. He felt infected everywhere; he felt watched. He worried about whether he ought to inform the nuns about his visitor. He stood loitering—now it was he who lurked and watched. The girl did not return—unless she was here now, waiting for his heavy odorous stream to strike the pail. It seemed to him finally that no girl had come down the stairs. A hallucination. He could inform the nuns of a hallucination. He counted fourteen meals before he told the breakfast nun (so orderly and predictable were they) that a Renée Le Fèvre had wandered into his hiding place. The nun kept up her unremitting smile: "She is our privilege. It is a privilege to invite you, Monsieur Brill, and also to invite this child." "Is she a Jew?" "She is of the same family as Our Lord." "She said she's a third-generation Catholic." "She is already beautiful in the faith. She wishes to be as we are, and we thank Our Lord for the gift of His blood through His seed of the flesh. Monsieur Brill, be calm. You are in no peril. She should not have come here, but you are in no peril." "If she speaks to the others?" "She is known to be a storyteller, Monsieur Brill. They say she fabricates. And what if a child fantasizes a very little bit? Put your soul at rest."

Safe on the tongue of a liar. But the next day all four of the nuns came to him. This was nothing ordinary. Sometimes two would descend together, one staggering under the big tin tub for his bath, the other with a great harsh towel and extra water jugs; from this he knew that another week had gone by, and also that it was the middle of the night. Four together signified a large event, as when he was first received into the convent. They had brought with them one of their own habits. They helped him into it (the smell of laundry soap and burning, the smell of the pyre) and led him upward through corridors and out an iron gate embossed with angry angels to a curtained car. It was bright day. The sun assaulted him; a blow on the eyeballs. He sat on plush so princely that he was certain this must be the car that follows the hearse. There was, however, no evidence of a funeral, almost no evidence of anything—only movement, and the brush of his own unaccustomed swathings, and the nuns' murmurs among themselves, shutting him out. They had urged him to take nothing with him. He said he would go as he had arrived: but he pushed into Rabbi Pult's briefcase, alongside the *Ta'anit*, a swiped copy of an early play by Edmond Fleg: *La Bête*. On the flyleaf there was inscribed a single word in the old priest's handwriting: *Délicieux*.

Through a chink in the curtains he saw Paris fly away: buntings, swastikas, but also the airy life of the streets as always. Sunlight! *Délicieux*. He envied the living and the free. He envied the dead and the free. In his long skirts and his flowing headgear he was feverishly afraid. They warned him to lie back, to keep his face from the window, to pretend to be sick and asleep, to cover himself with his veil. Somewhere in the suburbs they were stopped, checked, passed; then they turned into a leafy road and drove all day and into the night. He fell asleep in earnest and heard, repeatedly, a single sentence: *These are holy women.* The sentence seemed to refer not to the nuns, but to his sisters, the ABCs—were they dead, dying, captive, escaped? He thought he had lived no longer than two or three months in the subcellar of the convent. They told him it had been eight months; they delivered him to a farmhouse, removed his costume, and left him.

He spent the rest of the war in a hayloft. Sun, rain, weather; the furies of heat, a rimy cold so cruel his unwilled tears froze on his face. Restless animals below. Occasionally the danger of the veterinarian's visit; then he was locked in the toolshed, crouching among prongs and blades. They were not kind to him here—not that they were unkind, but they were gnarled and fearful old people, hardworking and childless, the husband with long leathery earlobes, the wife always suspicious inside her empty eyes, so pale they were almost white; they disliked him because he was the age a son of theirs might have been, had the woman not been barren. He saw what they thought about him: You live, and our son, only on account of not having been born, is dead. On lucky days he drank fresh cream or sucked on new peaches straight from the orchard. He raked manure and heaped it and mixed it with compost. He was allowed to make himself useful on condition that no part of him, not even his shadow, would ever be glimpsed by anyone. He flitted like a barn wraith, beginning to believe himself invisible. The subcellar, with its cot, its lamp, its cave of books, its meal-carriers and water-carriers—all of that struck him now as paradise lost. He defecated side by side with oxen. He ate what he found or filched. They gave him the husband's castoff overalls and a threadbare blanket—a corner of it was stiff with dried blood, animal or human. He felt himself more and more turning into a beast of the field, and it was increasingly curious to him (though now he never dared laugh out loud) that the one book, besides the *Ta'anit*, that he had brought away with him was called *The Beast*. He had lost his will to read. There were flickering spirals behind his eyes. He lay passively for hours, testing the edge of his winter hunger but sometimes not knowing what to do about it. He watched the glow of sunlight on the spiky hairs of the straw, or on the nervous ears, silky and cavernous, of the cows. The cows seemed to him more intelligent than the man and woman who were preserving his life. At night, when it was very cold, he climbed down the ladder and snuggled close to their swelled udders, between twin flanks, like a baby burrowing between a pair of breasts. He reminded himself that he was rid of *nox perpetua*; he knew when it was light and when it was dark. He had the diurnal cycle; he had the seasons. In the spring he bathed in a metal barrel that gathered rainwater, but it was full of leaves and twigs, and the mouth of it was crisscrossed with gummy spiderwebs. Once, at twilight, he ran squatting and stooping through a labyrinth of hayricks until he reached a brook. He splashed in with his clothes on. Bliss flowered in all his limbs. The water was icy and pure, tinged golden and black. There were velvet clots of emerald algae. He swam and he drank; he cleansed himself into wholeness, washing away the beast. That night the farmer entered the barn with a flashlight and the dwarfed but solid branch of a tree; he called Joseph down from the hayloft and said he had been seen in the brook by a child playing in the neighbor's meadow. Then he took the branch and felled Joseph with three violent slams.

All the same, he did not send Joseph away. He let him rake the barn, he let him hide—he never let him do any of the milking. The farmer's wife believed the milk would be cursed. Joseph's beard hung as low as his navel. His palms were as hard and dented as goat horns, and the nails of his fingers and toes were thick and jagged, like broken teacups. He was part ghost, part beast, part shard. He never once meditated on the intellectual union of Paris and Jerusalem. He was fixed on getting out of Europe; on leaving France; and sometimes, when he lay curled among bird droppings and the droppings of small rodents and bats, he dreamed of razing Paris to the ground—so that it would look like the brilliant meadows all around him, the wilderness of meadows that piled gold upon gold until they came to the lip of the brook.

After the war he found the ABCs alive, but no one else. His three older sisters had been scattered and starved; they had been caught and enslaved. They cared mainly about eating. But they were alert, ferocious. Berthe went immediately to England, to marry a British soldier she had met on the day of liberation; his family, originally from Minsk (Berthe cackled out the irony of it), owned a bakery in Manchester. She wrote letters thickened by scones, pies, currant buns, cream puffs, breads kneaded of rye, wheat, corn, malt. Anne and Claire straggled back to Paris and set up housekeeping together; Joseph moved in with them and returned to the observatory to learn that old Gaillard had died two months before, in his own bed, of pneumonia. Gaillard's successor took Joseph back; he treated Joseph like an intruder. Joseph did not mind.

He devoted himself to the study of the possibility of liquid nitrogen oceans on distant satellites; he puzzled over faraway fractures and vapors; he brooded about whether the rings of Saturn were electrically charged. He had re-entered civilization: then why did he feel desiccated? Why, stretching toward the margins of the remotest blue haze, did he judge himself to be middling? Through telescopes as huge as chimneys he looked toward the mathematical spheres. The radio emissions of orbs and powers and particles wheeled by in their shining dress. He was discovering himself not to be a discoverer—both too shabby and too cunning for the stars, so he abandoned his life to the chances and devisings of another continent.

He left his sisters, his degree, the observatory; he saw they were all middling. It was true, without Gaillard the observatory was middling; he left Paris. For the next thirty years he lived with a mediocre view of a children's playground in the middle of America. For all that time, and more, he lived, in fact, in a hayloft.

Joseph Brill's negotiations with the rich benefactress settled particularly on the question of the spacious but deteriorating stable situated several yards behind the old chair factory. The rich benefactress proposed converting the stable's broad lower floor into a gymnasium, and the hayloft over it into a snug Principal's Residence—i.e., a tiny apartment for Joseph. Joseph wanted the stable torn down. He said he was willing to find a place to live in a nearby suburb; he was willing to drive to the school every day. He was even willing to forgo a gymnasium, if it meant they could get rid of the hayloft: a playground would supply exercise enough. The rich benefactress was appalled at the notion of an American school without organized Physical Education. She would no more do without a gymnasium than without a blackboard in every classroom. Moreover, her idea of a Principal was one of what she called "steady accessibility." "In sight and on site," the rich benefactress expressed it. She had a billboard streak; she liked slogans. Rather romantically, she had only recently unearthed Joseph impecuniously teaching Hebrew school in a rundown synagogue in Milwaukee. This was, at least, the benefactress's view of it; she did not understand that Joseph had, with huge tenacity, inquired and inquired until *he* had unearthed the rich benefactress. Who, then, had chosen whom? Attraction fed attraction; beyond the mere contract, it was a compact. Though unprepossessingly penniless, Joseph was nevertheless favored with a sumptuous Parisian inflection. Its source was lost on the rich benefactress, whose own accent was marked by Bobruisk, a middling town in White Russia. The Eldorado opulence of the Rue du Faubourg St. Honoré and the steaming stalls of the Rue des Rosiers (swarming with an accent indistinguishable from the benefactress's own, only embedded in a kind of French) were all the same to her. It was the high muse of Europe she meant to snare. In the syllables of Joseph Brill—late of his father's fish store—she heard only the seductive antiquity of the oldest university. François Villon danced through Joseph Brill's nostrils. Philanthropy, dutiful and ambitious, would bring a shadow of the Sorbonne into being in the middle of America: a children's Sorbonne dense with Hebrew melodies, a Sorbonne grown out of an exiled Eden. The waters of Shiloh springing from the head of Europe!

"When my architect gets done with the place you'll never recognize it. You'd never know it was a hayloft. You don't have to act as if there's a devil in the deal. Tell you what," the rich benefactress said—she had the roused dowager authority of a woman who has been long and successfully widowed—"take the gym and the hayloft—your own apartment on the grounds—and I'll yield you a bargaining point on the name. I don't *like* the name, and if *I* haven't heard of Edmond Fleg, who has?" But she was drawn to everything Joseph explained about his idea for a Dual Curriculum. Chumash, Gemara, Social Studies, French: the waters of Shiloh springing from the head of Western Civilization!

By then Joseph Brill was thirty-one years old. His sister Berthe had divorced her soldier husband and returned, mockingly, to Paris. The ABCs were together again. They called Joseph a drifter: he had sacrificed the observatory to go to an obscure inland city in the country of illusion to become nothing at all.

He wrote them his victory: he crowed: he announced that he was now Principal Brill of the Edmond Fleg Primary School. He described the hayloft: "I'm to have a house on a lake." He described the school: "A sturdy brick fortress of a building, with a history of its own, to be renovated and modernized with every facility, including an up-to-date gymnasium." Claire wrote back and complained that his letter was a brochure: *they* weren't prospective pupils! Berthe wrote: "Joseph, you should marry." She enclosed a photograph of the ABCs: all were now shockingly overweight. Anne now did not write at all.

The classrooms were modestly but handsomely built; the old factory windows had been retained, tall and narrow, like slits in a castle tower: but the slits gave out on a wide glistening scene of water-blue and sky-white. A whole caravan of clouds progressed from window to window, nudging and snooping.

He lived in the hayloft. It was true it was no longer recognizable as a hayloft. But it remained dark and small. The floorboards groaned and dipped. No one called it the Principal's Residence; it was always "the hayloft."

Only the gymnasium was somehow never completed. The rich benefactress had reconsidered. Now she thought the money should be put to better use: it was already clear, given the fine introductory enrollment, that a new wing would soon be needed. The freshly planted playground below the hayloft—yellow swings, green slides, orange monkey bars: it made Brill think of tropical birds— was enough. To get to his apartment, Principal Brill had to pass through this playground, penetrate the black windowless breadth of the lower floor with its phantom horses, and approach a metal staircase along a cobwebbed rear wall. This useless dim space was gradually turning itself into a storeroom. There were already boxes of workbooks heaped up. It reminded him of the nuns: how they had kidnapped and abandoned him. He crossed through and climbed a short flight and came into a little kitchen the size of a library carrel or, more likely, a trough.

The younger children believed that the ghosts of horses stamped and neighed and steamed their breath under Principal Brill's bedroom floor in the middle of the night.

All the old names stuck—not just "the hayloft." The original factory building persisted in being called "the old section." And, though the new wing had been squatting there for twenty-six years, the most recent contingent of parents went on referring to it as "the new wing"; and so did Principal Brill.

The most recent contingent of parents were almost always surprised to be told that the rich benefactress was not dead. She was in fact abundantly aged, even hallowed; but she was also senile, traveling in a chrome wheelchair pushed by a male nurse in red sandals. Now and then, when a sparse wind of oxygen coughed in her brain, she ascended to lucidity, cradling a tape recorder in a blanket on her lap, dropping into it wavering bulletins: *Founded school . . . organized funding . . . inspired board of trustees . . . hired Joseph Brill bright moody boy from Paris, France . . . he drew up Curriculum. . . .* This self-righteous list—truncated, abrupt, grunted—exempted the rich benefactress from the Principal's secret cynicism: every item was truth.

Except for Commencement, the rich benefactress did not often appear on the grounds. But on Commencement night she sat in the dusk, pillowed and braced, a worn widowed old turtle in the shell of her chair: lidless, immobile. It was a long time since she had interfered in the school's affairs, though once she had threatened a parent with her plated reptile fist. She protected Brill always: there was an old war in the Edmond Fleg Primary School.

The war was between Principal Brill and the parents. By now it was well past the raging point; it was a tradition: an institution parallel with the institution of the school itself. The parents resented Brill. Some loathed him. Even his handful of admirers admitted that he was brilliance gone to seed, that his famous Dual Curriculum—one half concentrating on the Treasures of Western Culture, the other half given over, in their original tongues, to the Priceless Legacy of Scripture and Commentaries—had ossified. A splinter group insisted that there was nothing inherently malevolent in the Principal himself, only that he was an inferior pedagogue: he was unfit, he had aspirations but no system: even the thinnest theory ought to produce its technique. The origins of the war—what year it had begun, and over which issue—were forgotten; each side knew the other's tactics by heart. Both sides were engrossed by tactics. The mothers accused Brill of élitism. He retorted that he would not abandon the loftiest for the lowest. "I began as a stargazer," he would remind them, "and I will continue to look higher than the worm. *Ad astra!*"

But he scorned the mothers. "These *women*," he would say, and sometimes, in Yiddish, *"di vayber,"* as if the word had long been pickled in gall. A majority of the fathers were doctors. They were specialists in heart, kidney, liver, bones, blood, skin. One or two were psychiatrists. They were handsome, and disliked their elderly patients; they believed themselves immune to old age. They walked about with instruments clipped to their belts— the instruments were capable of emitting electronic birdcalls when activated from far away. *Cheep, cheep,* several of the instruments would cry out during a meeting of the Education Committee. Principal Brill did not honor these physicians; he thought them stingy. Their philanthropies were rare and grudging. The biology lab had never had even so much as a microscope from any of them. Instead, they owned sailboats, and at the annual fall picnic stepped out right onto the school beach, their belts cheeping over denim shorts and virile calves.

The mothers came to him in committees, in troops, in adversary eddyings; they came to quarrel. The old dismal combat crackled on. The math workbooks were geared to experts in advanced calculus, not to the fourth grade. The eighth grade, that race of giants, should not have had its lunch shift scheduled before the second grade, which got cranky when hungry. The vocabulary lists were too long. The teachers worked the children too hard, they expected too much. They did not work them hard enough, they expected too little. Brill knew how to hear the mothers out; they were not like Frenchwomen, he fathomed by now how their American impudence needed its sacrifice. Sometimes, when grimly pressed, in order to keep the peace he yielded outright, and fired a teacher in midterm.

The mothers' voices, surly, bold, powerful; he thought of them as egrets twittering over their nestlings. Their pants suits, their plumpness, their breasts, the secret hips of the slim ones, their long hair glistening downhill; he saw them as nature's creatures, by which he meant vehicles instinct with secretion: the pocket-mouth of the uterus, motherhood red in tooth and claw. Even when he yielded, he mastered them, because they had arrived as petitioners, as suppliants, and to yield was to consummate mastery—it was the sign of his scepter. The mothers had no humor, no irony, only fury. They beat on and on: my child; the other children; the teacher; the word lists; the homework. He saw how their anger was stimulated by the mammary glands. They were no more than antagonistic reflexes brewed in the scheme of the stars. Miniature cauldrons of solar momentum.

He felt himself their ruler; he was their god; their gleaming seated Buddha.

And shrunken all the same; he knew how shrunken. His learning was stale; by now everything was memory. He could still reel off lines from Baudelaire, or Rimbaud, or Mallarmé, or Verlaine, and every spring he invaded the sixth-grade room to write on the blackboard

Mais où sont les neiges d'antan?,

but he no longer seriously read. He never so much as yawned through the *Times*, not even on Sundays; he let lapse his dutiful subscription to *Le Monde*; instead, he bought the town paper, with its quick news of burglaries and local funerals—he liked to see which cans of vegetables were on sale at the A&P. He remembered the illuminations he had long ago undergone in steeping himself in this or that volume—rows and rows of Balzac, for instance; and *Madame Bovary*; and Proust, to the cadences of whose sentences he had once wed his heart's pulse. But now he dozed away nights in the shifting rays of lampless television, stupefied by Lucy, by the tiny raspy-voiced figures of the Flintstones; by the panic-struck void.

The void swarmed with nether voids: mirrors of voids: loss after loss. Many and much. He counted over the many: his father and mother; Michelle, Leah-Louise, Ruth; Gabriel and Loup; Rabbi Pult. The rest, the insubstantial much, was everything—his own tongue; the sumless sums that signified the galaxies; the other life, the Unknown, he might have endured had he not been born into the Middle, the sea of monsters that was—*coup de hasard*—his own time.

And he had no wife.

In late summer, before the new term opened, he said to Gorchak, "The school is honored. You won't believe whose child."

"Boy or girl?" Gorchak asked.

"The *mother*. It's a question of who the mother is."

"It's a question of whether the child is a good worker or lazy."

Ephraim Gorchak was the Principal's best teacher. He was the most reliable member of Brill's staff. He was always on time, never missed a day, and even the children felt how fair he was, especially in giving marks. It was easy for him to be fair, because his tests were all mechanical—either you knew the answer or you didn't—and all he had to do was add or subtract points. Each pupil knew how he stood with Gorchak. If you had high marks, you were a good worker, and Gorchak would respect you, which he showed by a kind of teasing. If you had low marks, you were a dimwit, and Gorchak would treat you as you deserved, looking past you as if he were affronted by the sight of you. He was a squat young man with a burning bush of a head: red brambles sprouted from behind his ears and neck. His thrust-out chin was slightly cleft, but the hollow was constantly being filled in by a fast-growing beard. His jowls were either orange or pinkish, depending on the intensity of the light: a bright dawn seemed perpetually about to break in his lower face, especially in mid-afternoon. He had flat pale eyes under slow lids, and an altogether pretty nose conscious of its duty.

Brill felt contempt for Gorchak, but he also valued him. Even though Gorchak was on the more difficult side of the Dual Curriculum, he was still a teacher in an elementary school, and Principal Brill knew better than anyone (better than the doctors, who accused him of obtuseness, cowardice, rigidity) what such people were. The women among them could never really be counted on: their cars broke down, their children got sick, or they themselves would catch cold. Worse, their classrooms were chaotic, disorderly. Gorchak's car never broke down, his children—a boy in third grade, a girl in fifth—were robust, his serene blue eyes never watered. Moreover, his classroom was perfectly disciplined. What disciplined it was ridicule. The ridicule came out of Gorchak's system of meticulous fairness: either you had the right answer or you did not. If you did not, Gorchak would make everyone see what a foolish answer it was. He would get everyone to laugh at you, and even you yourself, if you could manage not to cry, would laugh right along with the others.

Brill understood all this, but he recognized that it was healthful for the children to knead into the tension of the long Dual Curriculum day a fair sprinkling of levity, so he did not interfere. The laughter tumbled all morning out of Gorchak's classroom door, because Gorchak was impatient with error, and even more impatient with laziness. The first thing he told certain parents was to throw away words like "under-achievement" and "potential." Either a pupil was a good worker or he was lazy. A lazy pupil was a dreamer. The dreamers were worthless. Their heads were always drawn leftward, toward the windows; the green slope on that side of the school rose to meet the beach and the almost empty lake. Sometimes a sailboat pasted its white triangle against the silver water. Once a bird's tail brushed the windowpane like an upside-down broom. Gorchak's subject was Bible History. He kept up a military pace, one-two-three, too brisk for mooning out of windows. He taught all those stories just as they filed by in the text, but what he liked best was lists, especially of place names and journeys: *And they sojourned from the wilderness of Sin, and pitched in Dophkah. And they journeyed from Dophkah, and pitched in Alush. And they journeyed from Alush, and pitched in Rephidim, where there was no water for the people to drink.*

Gorchak asked, "Where was there no water to drink?"

Twenty hands beat upward: "Call on me, Mr. Gorchak! Please, please, Mr. Gorchak!"

"Michael!" Gorchak shot out.

"Rephidim!"

"Good, Michael, good!"

And on the next weekly test he would ask: "Name all the places the Children of Israel camped on the journey out of Egypt, from the Wilderness of Sinai on. Two points per correct answer."

The correct answers were: Kibroth-hattaavah, Hazeroth, Rithmah, Rimmon-perez, Libnah, Rissah, Kehelath, Mount Shepher, Haradah, Makeheloth, Tahath, Terah, Mithkah, Hahmonah, Moseroth, Bene-jaakan, Hor-haggidgad, Jotbath, Abronah, etc., etc. And when he returned the papers, striped all over with his large tidy check marks, Gorchak would say, "There was no reason for anyone not to get one hundred percent. All you had to do was learn the mimeographed list I gave you a few weeks ago. All you had to do"—and here he would give his special roguish look—"was remember to save that list just in case. If you didn't save it, it was plain laziness and I can't help you."

And again everyone laughed, because the special roguish look meant that he was pretending that he was not making a joke about the lazy pupils, whose names everyone knew, and there was nothing funnier than when Gorchak pretended nothing was funny. His pretty nose was perfectly bland, his face unmoved: dawn stopped in its tracks.

The Principal was proud that he had a teacher as popular as Gorchak, but at the same time it showed him his terrible isolation: he had no one who could understand the sensation that overcame him now and then, especially at Commencement. The graduation ceremony was very beautiful, always at the edge of evening, with the shining yellow arc of sand fading from its June butteriness to filmy gray to the kind of pink mirage that lasts only a fraction of a second before the depth of the true dark. Down the hill from the quick of the lake the eighth grade liquidly drifted, first the girls in their white dresses, holding their little bouquets or garlands, like a flock of brides, and just behind them the boys subdued by their stiff new navy-blue suits, trailing after the amazing bright bevy of those mass brides. Mainly it was during these moments that Principal Brill felt the wild awfulness of the sensation: but sometimes he felt it when he peered into the first-grade room, and heard all those little ones reciting; or the pang would snap against his liver when he saw even one child, a new child who was being interviewed, with the mother sitting close.

The interview consisted of his holding up five fingers.

"How many?" the Principal asked.

"Five," the child murmured.

Now again he held up five fingers, but also the thumb of the other hand. "How many now?"

The child sunk her head into her collar.

"Now?" he persisted.

The tender head stayed down. The child did not reply. He took in, with no reservations, that she was not one of the bright ones, and just then the pang, the sensation, the almost-animal that ran its warm paws alongside his liver, made him know again his condition: his discovery. His condition was immortality. His discovery was its horror. He did not attempt to draw Gorchak into this cold knowledge: how year after year it was the same, the first-graders so tender-mouthed and little, the eighth-grade girls exploded into puberty, the candle-tips of their breasts puffed up beneath their white dresses in the long procession down the glowing hill; spring after spring after spring. Nothing moved. Nothing altered. The first grade was always the first grade, the eighth grade always the eighth. This knowledge turned him cold; it was the coldness of the cosmos itself. The same, the same, the same. For this the nuns had kept him alive. For this the hayloft had kept him alive. Nature replaces, replaces identically, replaces chillingly.

He feared for himself, because he was of the elect, the fearful elect who are swallowed up by a look at immortality. The look flashed in him often and often. He saw how he had not died in the middle of the time of dying. And then he saw how they would continue to pass before him, these children who were eternally children, who could never grow beyond the age of pubescence; they passed before him, always the same, always the same: the same timid ones, the same wags and cutups, the same eyes with their hidden hurts, the little beauties, the mournful unblessed, the whole ragbag of by and large indifferently formed flesh thrust from the legs of the newest batch of mothers. Wave after wave, and always the same wave. They were like the stars that are still alive, or possibly dead. You are not permitted to witness their endings; only, carried by antique light, their earliness.

To Gorchak he said again: "The mother."

"Whose mother?" Gorchak said.

"The mother of the child I interviewed today." And for some

reason—it was not impulse, but he had no clear purpose in doing it—he handed over to Gorchak Dr. Glypost's report. Dr. Glypost was the school psychologist, though in reality the school had no such factotum on a regular basis, as other schools had. It cost too much. Dr. Glypost was an autumn hireling; just before the start of each new term she tested the incoming pupils for disturbance, neuroses, left-handedness. She distinguished between the worthwhile and the worthless. She weeded out. She was vain about her credentials; her judgment had no elasticity. Like Gorchak, she saw only success or failure. Her pride in her education led her to predict and command the future.

Gorchak read:

BEULAH LILT, AGE FIVE YEARS ELEVEN MONTHS

Beulah is a tense, anxious child, constricted in her approach to tasks, lacking in spontaneity, withdrawn in her relationships to others. Though she is right-handed, she is not well-integrated and she did not use the testing time in an efficient or assured manner. There is a rigidity about her and a weakness in adaptability. She sat through the entire testing period without smiling once. She was slow, like a sleepwalker. She had dead eyes. Shown a Rorschach card expressing ominous darkness, she responded with Storm Cloud. The popular response among children of her age is Bird or Bat. Non-achiever, not recommended for Dual Curriculum.

Gorchak said soberly, "You didn't admit this child?"

"She's already registered."

"And the interview with you? She did better with you?"

"She was afraid. Paralyzed. She couldn't add five and one."

"She'll fail," Gorchak said. "Not a good worker. Slow is lazy. She gave the wrong answer. The good workers said Bird or Bat."

Brill said, "I can't let her slip through my fingers."

"She'll drag down the school average. She'll dream," Gorchak warned.

"I am mindful of our reputation," Brill said. "She'll polish it up for us. A luminary. She'll do us good. I can't let her slip." He took in the elegant turn of Gorchak's nostrils and said, "I mean the mother. You don't know the mother." He had not expected Gorchak to know the mother. He plucked back Dr. Glypost's report and shoved it into a folder. "Dr. Glypost is a grid. The holes are large and crude. It would be a detriment to the honor of the school if we let her slip through one of Dr. Glypost's abysses."

Principal Brill's teachers were like children themselves. He was familiar with their habits. Family, cooking, television, good marks. They had all had good marks in elementary school. They taught "respect for books," but they wrote childish memos (even their handwriting was childish) and, though they had by heart the causes of the War of 1812, they were ignorant. They all had a certain childish liveliness.

"Hester Lilt," he told Gorchak. "The mother is Hester Lilt."

"I think I've heard of her," Gorchak said.

Brill knew he had not.

S he was an imagistic linguistic logician, a phrase foreign to Brill. He had no idea of its purport. But he had seen her interviewed on a television program, and that was what they had called her then: an imagistic linguistic logician. A mouthful. Though Brill recollected the name of her most celebrated book, *The World as Appearance* (*"die Welt als Erscheinung,"* a Kantian borrowing), he had not read it or any of the four others. He took them all out of the local public library. Eventually he would send away to the publisher and buy them; they demanded long reflection. One was called simply *Mind*, but when he looked again, he saw the subtitle: *Ancient and Modern*. The three others were *Metaphor as Exegesis, Divining Meaning*, and *Interpretation as an End in Itself*.

He turned the pages of the last. "The eternal concurrent of language," he read, "is the shadow of language, by which we intend its effect; language without consequence, i.e., the 'purity' of babble, is inconceivable in the vale of interpretation." It made him feel weak.

But when she came to him about the child she spoke plainly, in a commonplace way; you could not tell from her voice, her manner, her blouse, what she was. In the window of the little box near his bed she had seemed older, white-haired, great bleak wells under the eyes; at least sixty. In his office he saw she was perhaps ten years younger than that, with a wide face, a fat-weighted chin, and thick strands of jagged hair always on the loose, wandering aloft; sticking up or out. He felt the faintest prong of recognition. Her shoes were well worn—he didn't recognize *those*. No one had ever sought him out with shoes like that. Even on the surface she was different from the other mothers because, he surmised, she did not go to a hairdresser or contemplate her clothes. Her shoes were laced as well as old, and on this occasion she wore anklets, like an adolescent; her shins were too wide. All the same, the nagging of some nameless familiarity went on humming in a muted patch of his mind: a distant vibrato. Then she confirmed that she had appeared for the second time on the Public Education channel, late at night, only a month ago; so he thought it was from that.

It troubled him—it had never troubled him before—that the school's financial forms were premised on the husband as head of the family, as breadwinner, as the one responsible for writing the checks; she had no husband. She did not volunteer whether she was divorced or widowed. Her accent, in which Brill heard unknown segments of Europe, mystified him. So did her age. Was she forty-five, fifty? An elderly primipara—though the Principal had once read that Samuel Johnson's mother had borne him in her forty-first year: such women were not unusual among the hardy English. Brill looked into the logician's face—an instrument for assessing, measuring, taking in, it seemed well used rather than merely old—and wondered who had sired the child. Some bohemian vagabond? Another philosopher? Her own twin, a refugee survivor from Mittel-europa? He could neither charm nor intimidate her. She was neither forward nor quarrelsome. But her foreignness—it was not excessive—gave her away. It suggested her surrender at least: they were, after all, he and she, in the middle of America, connected by that other Middle, the true and horrific Middle, the Middle of their time, of which the intact and impregnable Americans understood nothing. He apprehended what it was that lay in her: a brokenness. She could never fool him. She was a looking-glass for him, and he was surely capable of staring straight into it.

Across his desk, over the mottled globe of the Bristol chair, he handed her the forms. He said, "Is it possible we're countrymen, Mrs. Lilt?"

"No," she said.

"But I thought I heard . . . Then Brussels? Zürich?"

"No. I'm not what you are."

"What am I?" he asked. He knew what he was. It was not a proper inquiry for an interview. In thirty years he had never put such a question to anyone.

"An American."

Slippery. Out of the blue. In two sentences she had backed him away and exposed him. He disliked irony. He disliked it that she withheld homage, solidarity, even plain comfort. He expected her to recognize him as he had recognized her. He saw that they were unfailingly alike, members of the same broken band, behind whose dumbshow certain knowings pace and pitch.

"And you?" he said. "You don't consider yourself an American? You're not an American now?"

"I've become what I intended to be."

This hurt him. It meant that he had not. The fallen astronomer. He tried to draw her out. She gave him little: she had left
the middle of Europe long ago, decades back, on one of those
Children's Transports, but he could not discover from what beginning she had been rescued. In nationality she seemed to be a bit
of everything; it was the brush of his native consonants he thought
he had momentarily heard. He listened in vain for her earliest
place. She said she had lived in London for years, had once
studied in Stockholm, had actually accepted a post in New Zealand
for a time, and was in fact only just lately considering another in
Paris; but this she would turn down, at least for now, because of
the child. Consistency. The child needed a spot, a school, a
constancy.

It was her single mention of the child. After that she had
nothing to say of the child. It was not like talking to a woman; it
was hard for him to think of her as a woman. She kept her neck
steady; she did not twist it around to show off her eyes, as so many
of the mothers did. Even her voice was a man's voice: full and
low. "I prefer," she told him in that dark barbed growl, "the lump
sum." He was taken aback by this directness. She had not been
willing to satisfy him about her history, but about money she was
clear enough. He was not used to a woman speaking so directly,
and he was not used to discussing tuition with one of the mothers.
"That's not how we do it," he explained. She was forcing him to
explain. He was not used to explaining, in a plain flat unquarrel-
some way, to one of the mothers. "We space it out. We require
postdated checks over a period of nine months." And for the first
time, when he said "nine months," although he had spoken this
very sentence a hundred times before to the fathers, he realized
its other meaning, the period of gestation, and his face and his
belly heated up.

She put her signature at the bottom of the form. He had never
encountered a woman's signature that was so like a man's. He
went on gazing at it. He had expected the usual female hand—
its frivolous slanting letters, the curves of the base strokes like

perfume reduced to hieroglyph, the cosmetic artifice of writing given over only to decoration; the trivialization of alphabet under a woman's fingertips.

She saw how he seemed to brood. "Did I sign in the right place?"

"Yes, yes, it's all in order." They shook hands. "The school," he said, "is honored." Again he considered her signature. *Lilt.* He imagined lutes. But no; undoubtedly a Hebrew origin. *Leyl,* night. Lutes of the night; night-music. Or that succubus to small boys in the ghetto, Lilith the night-demon. Her name made his throat swell. Its syllable was too brief; it passed him by too quickly. He wanted to detain her until he could learn what there was in her of *déjà vu.* He had viewed her before, and not only in the night glass of television. He pressed: "Will you come and speak?"

"Speak?"

"To the parents. We have a most distinguished parent body, numerous physicians, an annual luncheon—"

"What could I possibly speak about?"

"Something like on that last television program. You could talk on the condition of the—the dreaming rationalist."

"The dreaming rationalist?"

As if these weren't her own words! He felt that he was being made a fool of by all these echoings, but he temporized: he had his need. "My dear lady, it's not every day we have a parent like yourself. It's not every day that I can sit here and entertain a primary thinker."

"Mr. Brill"—she was stripping him; no one said his name without the plosive preface of his title!—"a contract isn't an entertainment and I'm not a primary thinker. Since Aristotle all thinkers are secondary."

"Dear lady, you meditate, you write—" He reached for the heap of library books on the far side of his big desk. "This one passage in particular, from *Divining Meaning,* you could address yourself to it perhaps—"

He read aloud:

When we think about thinking, we find ourselves in a position of self-justification. We are not willing to admit that we do not generate our own thoughts, but that, on the contrary, they appear to be generated *for us*, as if by a transcendent engine that connects the process of mind to some outward source, so that we have the sensation we are being *fed*, as in the expression *fed ideas*.

He asked, "Are there religious overtones to that?"

"Doubtless there are religious overtones to everything." She gave him her first smile now, which stretched her lips while hiding her teeth and oddly deepening a shallow cut in the flesh between the eyebrows. "You're acquainted with André Neher? He writes about Fleg—and Fleg's your rubric, isn't he? Your main skysail and masthead? You should read, in your own language, *L'Exil de la Parole*." He did not have to wonder whether the smile was satiric. She was patronizing him. It was a long time since he had had a conversation of this sort: himself not in control. Decades, perhaps. No one had spoken to him like this since Claude. She was clever enough to include even the sailboats on the lake. He had no idea who André Neher was; it was unlikely he would ever find out; he observed nevertheless that she uttered this name, and those few vocables of French, with a clear perfection. In the whole middle of America, there was no one with authority over so much. He was himself in exile from the word—incarcerated by night among phantom horsehoofs, indentured to ignorant teachers, the mothers, the doctors, the mental brutishness, the children; the perilous and shining Phlegethon.

It fell on him then—it might have been because of the clarity she brought to *parole*, the word that meant word: was she, for who knew what unhappy reason, concealing a birthplace along the Seine?—it fell on him that he recognized her from his own childhood. That chin, that nose! She had grown older, much older. She was changed. It was plain to him that she could no longer tantalize with her aristocratic small mouth, curled up—he saw through all that now. But the lute-voice—the lilt!—of French in her mouth wheeled her back to him: he felt the vertigo of it. There she was. She was white-haired and middle-aged and without a single pearl. But there she was—he knew her exactly—Madame de Sévigné! She had the face, the voice, the poise, the enigma of her character, the brilliance of her written sentences; the same stout neck. The only thing missing was that insanity about the daughter. Hester Lilt had no madness of that kind—she did not so much as say her daughter's name. The daughter was omitted. You could almost not tell she *had* a child. Yet who would ever have heard of the pampered sulky Comtesse de Grignan if not for the Comtesse's stupendous mother, purring and purring over her wholly unextraordinary *fille*? Madame de Sévigné without daughter-obsession: it could not be. Already the resemblance was waning. A fleeting aberration of his own, set off by the pure bell of the mother-tongue cleanly striking. Among all these children he longed for the child Joseph he had once been. She was not Madame de Sévigné. The portrait was immensely far off, in the Musée Carnavalet, inside another century, and even more distant, folded among the gossamer after-school dusks of the roundabout way. He understood that the wish for boyhood was a simple-minded wish for the return of beauty and burnished hope.

He looked up: recognition had vanished altogether. She was not like anyone. She had no double. She was serene. She was still patiently sitting with her sinister little perplexity of a smile. She was indifferent; he deserved her indifference. He marveled that he had imagined, even for the breadth of a moment, a likeness. Madame de Sévigné in the middle of America, on the lip of the Phlegethon!

"If you consider us hoi polloi," he argued barrenly, "and won't talk to the parent body, then how can I account for having seen you on television?"

"*Chaos ex machina.* An apparition," she offered.

He said glossily, "Your fame accounts for it, then. You can't avoid it. They come and drag you away."

"People like myself are never famous"—keeping up the mild, perplexing, dangerous smile.

"People like yourself never notice when you are." He had spun himself out to the limits of his courtliness. What she said was true. Gorchak did not know her name; fame is what the schoolteachers know.

He began to study her work in earnest. It was difficult to say whether it had "religious overtones"; sometimes it seemed to; sometimes not. He entered her mind; it was very serious in there, and very splendid; it made him afraid to encounter such a majesty of assimilation. She was right to admit she was not a primary thinker—it struck him that her ideas had a familiar cast. He had stumbled on some of them years ago, through Claude, in the days of his emancipation. He wondered whether she had a degree from anywhere. She did not call herself "Doctor," but this might only have been her pride, or else her abnegation, or else the sign of her solitude. Her consonants in English pricked like barbed wire. It came to him, turning and turning those rare pages, that she might have been a poet; but she had relinquished everything lyrical, everything "expressive." She renounced originality. She was only exact. She dealt in scrutiny and commentary. Her genius for clarity frightened him. He was intimately persuaded that she was honest. Not one lie. She was too logical to lie.

He had not applied himself in this way for a long time. He thought it would tire him, but instead it woke him up. Even while asleep he had alert dreams. He dreamed of strapping himself into the high riding-seat of the telescope at Mount Palomar, and being swung by machinery up, up toward the vast mirror, like a goddess's eye, that sucked in the reflections of the stars. In that immense looking-glass he revived the calm flat image of Hester Lilt's smile; he knew he had no status with her. This seemed just. He had absolved himself from his "potential"—why? Gorchak would deem it laziness. He argued to himself that he had abandoned astronomy because France was the land of his captivity, because France had been his Egypt. Then he was reminded that Ptolemy had been an Egyptian, and that Joseph in Egypt had made himself great. So it was not astronomy he had given up on, but greatness. He had forsaken the universe not because he was no good at it but because others were better. The heights or nothing. He was maddened by genius. He respected nothing else. Year after year he searched among the pupils. They were all ordinary. Even the brightest was ordinary. In three decades he had not found a single uncommon child. The best were like Gorchak, devoted to high marks.

In the school he felt his status. When he walked into a classroom, a stiffness, a reverence, came into the teacher. Or she might all at once turn jolly and make a joke, but that too was out of reverence. Mrs. Seelenhohl, for example, whom he knew to be a timeserver of the first water, rarely gave tests because she could not bear the labor of grading them, but the moment he appeared, she would announce a quiz for the very next day. Meanwhile he went into the first-grade room. Mrs. Bloomfield was there, indistinguishable from any of the young mothers. She had long brown hair. He had hired her on account of the precision of her speech. Very rapidly he learned she was stupid. He thought to himself: For the first grade, what does it matter? They manage eventually to read by themselves anyhow. The children were writing in their workbooks. He looked for Beulah Lilt. She was in a corner seat, in the row farthest back. She was holding a pencil and workbook. She was fixed on air, beyond the tall window, toward the sails. He strode over to her.

"What do you see out there?"

Her eyes shot down to her book.

"Something interesting?" It was his elfin way. He intended to be cheerful and teasing, and he saw that he really was—the whole room laughed, the high and rugged beast-laugh of small children. Beulah sat dumb. Abnormal. She could not be joshed. What could one do with a child like that?

He beckoned Mrs. Bloomfield out into the corridor. She ran forward with her long hair flowing, her widened nostrils tense. She was afraid of him. Always, with the teachers, he felt his power. He was their king. He said, "The Lilt child."

"Which one is that?"

Two weeks into the term, and she did not yet know Hester Lilt's daughter. "The blonde, with curls. The one I just spoke to."

"Oh that one." A grimace. "That one's hopeless. A deaf-mute. She doesn't talk. She never volunteers."

"Is she learning to read?"

"I've put her in with the slow beginners."

The child of Hester Lilt! He grieved at such incongruity. He knew himself to be a voyeur of early intellect; he longed for a child of genius to watch. Math or chess or cello. A prodigy. Youthful astronomer, what he himself had been; then backed away and began to drift. "Drifter," his sisters in chorus called him; Berthe especially. Berthe was the instigator. The heights or nothing. The loftiest ranges, from which he permitted himself to parachute, drifting downward—the school, its bestowal, his second chance, his turning, after Gaillard, after the nuns, after the hayloft, a life-shock: to seize in the hand new mind, fresh clay, early intellect, to begin again, to watch, to watch, and all in three boxcars on the shore of the Phlegethon; and he the boxcars' monarch. And then the blessed renewing days of his invention, the Dual Curriculum, the confluences of Edmond Fleg, the old priest's crates, the odor of subcellar and nuns' tapers—the inspiration, morning after summer morning, of fitting in this and fitting in that. Strange and shaming that it gave him happiness, or at least elation—it was a kind of archaeology: the digging down, the stone steps, Pult's briefcase, Le Fèvre born Levin, Jerusalem athwart the Louvre, the dream of founding a school, hallucination after hallucination, and all the while his bleating baby sister Ruth in the Vél d'Hiv, Pult breathing gas in Poland, his losses, his losses. He had come clean away, besmirched, the Dual Curriculum his bosom's only constancy. It was, in the end, a scheme of learning luminous enough for a royal prince or princess. But no prince or princess had ever been enrolled. He had no one worthy of his construction: lordly civilization enmeshed with lordly civilization, King David's heel caught in Victor Hugo's lyre, the metaphysicians Maimonides and Pascal, Bialik and Keats, Gemara hooked to the fires of algebra. Instead he was educating commoners, weeds, the children of plumbers. Plumbers: his name for the doctors, why not?

"The mother is exceptional," he instructed Mrs. Bloomfield; Mrs. Bloomfield was a reader of magazines bought on cashier lines at the supermarket. Hester Lilt's work must fall on Mrs. Bloomfield's cranium with no felt weight.

"You don't need a crystal ball to know about this one. Nothing much there, nothing much to come," Mrs. Bloomfield said.

"Could you try harder," he intoned. "Because of the mother."

"It's not the mother who's in my first grade." Was this defiance? She did not falter. "Principal Brill"—it *was* defiance—"you want a silk purse out of the wrong animal's ear."

"Get her reading," he threw behind him.

In his new wakefulness, his brain in friction, he telephoned the author of *Metaphor as Exegesis*. Her voice in response was croaky. He imagined her at work all night, her head lifted up only at dawn. "Did I wake you? Have I interrupted? Are you in concentration?" he asked, his blood beating with anxiety. All his American life he had been subject to infatuations. He recoiled from "appropriate" women. For thirty years the school mothers had been arranging marriages for him; and for the fulfillment of this gratifying aim even his worst enemies among the parents came forward with a generosity, a capaciousness, a monstrousness of good will. He had been deposited at this dinner table and that with a Miss Springer, a Miss Whitehill, a Miss Trittschuh, a Miss Tepperbaum. As a consequence he allowed the Rumor to emanate that long ago, during his student days, he had lost a sweetheart to tragic disease, desolating fate. They were soon to be engaged. His heart broke and he suffered without surcease. Thus the Rumor. Vapors of some forlorn Magic Mountain veiled it; or else the black gleam of short French cigarettes, the lung's blight. A fall from a high-legged horse, with cascading mane: broken neck, severed spine; her long, long coma. No one was sure of these tales. For Brill they all had the gauzy sliding wink of Claude. Who had brought them into being? Was it himself? Sometimes the Rumor took another shape: his sweetheart, a brave slender girl, member of the Resistance, heroine with code name, slips into England in the very hour of the blitz; she is crushed in the bomb-blown rubble of London's East End. Claude's ghost was not in that one. It was Principal Brill's heavy sister Berthe, her truncated Manchester marriage.

A romantically-minded minority party among the mothers accepted the Rumor, in all its transmutations, as an eternal predicament for a young, and then for a middle-aged, bachelor; but most knew it was absurd: time heals, he was stubborn, deceitful, evasive, spiteful, hopeless; a hopeless case. The Misses Springer, Whitehill, Trittschuh, and Tepperbaum, schoolteachers with their M.A.s in Nursery Education—pleasant-faced, thick-thighed girls enthralled to have met a real Frenchman, a Parisian with a degree from the Sorbonne, the head of a school—floated off, passed him by, displaying their reluctance in phantom murmurings: "He had a sweetheart killed in the blitz," they would say; or they would say, "She belonged to the Resistance, she was shot in a cellar"; or they would say, "She had to pose as a nun in order to stay alive, they gassed her in a Polish sports stadium," going offstage in their prime, generation after generation, while his brow widened and a white foam scribbled at his temples.

One day he saw he was older than he had ever been before, and that, though he had stayed in one spot for thirty years, he was exactly what his sisters took him for: a drifter. "You ought to get that Dr. Glypost to do one on *you*," his sister Claire wrote in the same letter that reported Berthe's second marriage, to a Hungarian refugee named Glassman: Berthe was in luck, he had a small shoe factory just outside of Paris—the slipper fit at last! And now the mothers began to fix Brill up with the less appropriate: widows getting on toward plumpness, with grown children; nervous divorcées, scratching at their little moles; secretaries and nurses who would not mind an older man because, they supposed, having spent his years in such a green and watery and airy landscape, he was rich. Gradually he fell into his great sleep, his head at the dinner table patient and somber; but unseen inside his skull he clicked his gold molar, unseen under the table his toes twitched in his shoes; with eyes wide he was somnolent. So they left him alone finally. Nights he lay down beside the flickering planetary glow of the television, sick with infatuation.

Brill's infatuations were terrible. They were also secret—trancelike, heavy. One summer, in such fine costly boots with shining nails, he toiled up a New England alp and at the top of it met a Unitarian minister and his wife. In the hotel the three struck up a friendship, arguing the historicity of the Patriarchs, then of Jesus; the wife, always out of breath, panting faintly in a way that ravished, pleaded so passionately for the actuality of the Saviour that he could not resist her round violet eyes and thick charcoal eyebrows lifted at their farther ends in almost an Oriental flourish. For two years Brill and Mrs. Carstairs corresponded. She was an Australian married to an American; the minister's congregation was in Labrador, Iowa. Brill was then forty, Mrs. Carstairs fifty-one. She had no children. "My dearest Mrs. Carstairs," he wrote in his last letter, growing breathless to match her, "it would be my joy to instruct you in the Holy Tongue. I would put each stroke and shape of the Hebrew alphabet into the palm of your hand like a most fragrant and rosy-colored pomegranate, a *rimon*. . . ." She did not reply to this offer. Two mornings before his letter arrived, her heart fanned, stirred, slowed, became as agitated as a cricket; then dropped into the cage of death.

All his infatuations were caged, breathless, fruitless, in the air: figments. A woman seen through a hairdresser's window, the white face floating all alone above a cloudlike vast bib, a silver bullet encasing the crown of the head, and only the profile revealed, in an isolation of perfection, of sweetness, a chin so cleanly arched that it might have sprung from the neck of a field flower. Or: a dancer glimpsed at a concert—not performing; it was a chamber-music concert to which he had escorted a Miss Feibush. Brill had not paid for the tickets. The school mother who had fixed him up with Miss Feibush had presented them to him as a gift: Miss Feibush was musical. He thought it a burden and a nuisance, the drive into the city with Miss Feibush chattering melodically at his side, sweating ever so slightly and giving off a perfume that, so he felt, was causing his bile to flow in the wrong direction. Miss Feibush was a social worker, and believed that Mozart, early urged on deprived children, enabled them to overcome the psychological maimings that are the consequence of economic impoverishment. Brill heard all these words and wanted to smack her. Her vocabulary was even more offensive than her sweat. At the concert Miss Feibush turned to him and pointed to a young black woman three rows behind them—how like her, to have swiveled her head backward! "That's Dyduma Mbora," Miss Feibush whispered; "don't you recognize her from that article?" Brill did not. "She's that Nigerian dancer on tour, you know the one, from that article in *Time*." He swiveled his own head and took in the molded brow of the African, her long throat wound in a tiger-striped shawl, her powerful knees staring forward nakedly at him like two fists. Without warning—and yet he was not excessively surprised—the first thwack of infatuation struck his Adam's apple, his stomach swarmed with too many organs, twin hearts and triple kidneys. Physiology menaced him. How he longed to follow her to Africa, to fold himself into knife blades of equator-heat for the sake of her wood-brown cheeks and berry-dark lips and polished mahogany thighs!

All these insubstantial mismatchings—woven of cloud and chimera—he attributed to the strangeness, the duality, of his own heart. Two worlds split him. A school that teaches Chumash and Rashi and Gemara is called a yeshiva; its head is called the Rosh Yeshiva. Whereas he, in his mock-Sorbonne, was a Principal and ran a Dual Curriculum. It could be done and yet it could not be done. Rather, it could be done only in imagination; in reality, it was all America, the children America, the teachers America, the very walls of the chair factory America. Egalitarianism—the lowest in the lead. And therefore all things lost to any hope of the patrician, himself the betrayer of Edmond Fleg. To the mothers he did not speak of Fleg; instead he drew them on feelingly with the dutiful phantoms of his dearest *Tantes*—how poignantly in this word the Yiddish and the French converged, how his *Tantes* together cried out into the crevasse of the icy planet: in the syllables of *Tante* itself there lurked the very crystals of the Dual Curriculum! "Two aunties nurtured me," he often explained, "my Torah *Tante* and my Parisian *Tante*, each the heiress of an ancient line." And then he would weave the "atmosphere" of each, the Talmud auntie analytical, exegetical, an extraordinary cogitator, energetic chessmistress and mistress of many-layered syllogism, problem-inventor-and-unriddler, at the same time a softie, merciful, her bundles tumbling and tears often in her eyes; the Paris auntie, though herself very old, nevertheless aeons younger than the Talmud auntie, and rather more callous, a bit cold, her glory in her raiment and manner, lofty and lean, with a long distinguished chin like a young comte's, her gaze an ascent of gargoyled spires and her lips overflowing with Baudelaire. "From these two *Tantes*," he would say (using the French intonation) in those theatrical moments when his fingertips plucked the air like notes on a staff and charm rang its music in his running voice, "I derived my inspiration for the Dual Curriculum." He omitted Edmond Fleg—no matter that the school bore that uncharted name! He omitted the sweet fumes of the nuns, the old priest's pen-dappled volumes. He omitted his hidden life. His voice was handsome and large as well as occasionally puckish. The vowels were humble in their foreignness, their timbre benevolently royal—clad in lace.

Hester Lilt was not an infatuation; he was almost sure of this. She was too hard on him, and also too easy; she was indifferent. "Allow me to apologize," he said into the telephone, "I've been reading you and you are quite right, our parent body would not be able to follow you. My intention—I confess it—was to exploit you." He stopped; she breathed serenely on. "To attract notice. Glory and honor to the school. You know I used to be an astronomer. If I asked you to come to us in a public way, it's only because I am still in pursuit of the stars."

He was pleased with this conceit: it was how he addressed the elderly benefactress. Or, when he spoke at Commencement, peering brazenly into the meadow covered and multicolored by the assembly of parents: "The whole host of heaven is here tonight. I'm glad to tell you that as a former astronomer"—and here he would lift an arm toward the glimmering Phlegethon and the graduates arrayed above it—"I am particularly fit to recognize risen angels." Or, at the close of an especially bitter meeting with the mothers: "Ladies, I submit. You see in me a pale satellite shot

molds, to bring form into being. He acknowledged—now that he was looking for it—how she worked to make a frame for every idea. Her ideas were peculiarly athwart, as if in parody. She set out—she mimicked—every rational scheme, but with the almost imperceptible screw-turn of her malignant smile. He had witnessed that smile only once, and for only a moment; but retrospectively, toiling through her work, he learned the quality of its tight-stretched mirth. It was strange to think she had a child. Profoundly, illimitably, he knew the mothers; she was not like any of them. The unselfconscious inexorable secretion ran in all of them. From morning to night they were hurtled forward by the explosions of internal rivers, with their roar of force and pressure. The mothers were rafts on their own instinctual flood. Encirclement, preservation, defense, protection: that was the roar and force. That was why they lived, and how: to make a roiling moat around their offspring. The ardor of their lives was directed toward nothing else, and though it seemed to be otherwise, they were in the pinch of nature's vise, they were contained in an illusion of freedom: as the bee in midflight is unaware its purpose is honey, and supposes each flight to be for flight's sake, so the mothers went here and there, and did this and that, and believed one thing and another, but all for an immovable and unsubtle end. And their offspring too would one day be the same: aggressive, arrogant, pervicacious: the gland's defense of the necessary shove toward continuity.

This was his own view, though certain of the words were not: for instance, the image of the bee duped by its own behavior was Hester Lilt's. To his astonishment he found himself in her audience, before a platform on which she sat with two others. It was not a large auditorium, but it was well stocked with faces pushing forward, lit and straining. He saw she had her little following. It was a "symposium"; the topic was "An Interpretation of Pedagogy." All this came to him in a note. He marveled that she had thought of him, that it seemed worthwhile to her to invite him. Her single sentence, in that unwomanish hand, was abrupt enough:

"Mr. Brill: I intrude on your demesne," succeeded by the place and time and that peculiar subject. Again she withheld his title. The word "demesne"—how shrewdly and cruelly chosen. Plainly she recognized his narrow reality, his tiny kingdom, his scepter the width of a thread, his diminutive sovereignty. The Little King. She recognized all this and meant to taunt.

All the same, he turned up. The meeting was in a room at the state university. He drove to the far side of the city, and then beyond into unfamiliar villages—though he had set out in sunlight, night overtook him—and soon lost himself in the parking lots of the campus, blundering from field to field. He left the car and began to search on foot in the blackness. A guard led him into the right building at last, but sent him down the wrong corridor. Altogether he was an hour late and had missed all the keys to the proceedings—who these two hairy men on the platform were, who these leaning and hard-breathing listeners were, what manner of fellowship he was witnessing. It rapidly came to him, then, that she had intended not merely a taunt but a reprimand. Captain of fleas and midges, warrior among the mothers! She meant him to feel his shame and denigration: how had he dared to ask her to speak to his little pond, his mothers, his doctors? Each of the two hairy men—hair fallen on the forehead, hair scrabbled over the ears, hair springing upward from the wrists, the lip, the jowl—called the other an "epistemologist." One had an enormous belly, a funerary mound pouting between short legs. The other kept winding and unwinding his ankles behind his calves. But their hands lay like sleeping infants in their laps, they were clement and content, and even when in disagreement failed to argue. Brill presently understood why. They were an alliance in thrall to Hester Lilt. They were no more than a chorus behind her, while she, between them, reading aloud from a gray sheet, was clearly the point of the occasion. He heard her voice as if separated from its freight, a sound dark and darting, almost too mobile, though edged with a certain scrape among the lighter vowels (hints of an

undisclosed geography, her own hidden life), and this alone was
so interesting to him that it was a long while before he could pay
attention. When he did, she was absorbed by a phrase: "the unsurprise of surprise": she was telling how in Mozart, and in Thomas
Mann (she had other illustrations as well, but those were not
known to him), the sudden lifted note, the upward slope of the
arch of narration, arrive to widen one's eyes with the shock of first
encounter; but only seconds afterward, when the resolution has
been drilled through, the note, and the arch itself, seem predestined, the surprise seems natural and predictable. From this she
rapidly passed into what Brill soon affirmed to himself must be an
assault on psychology, fragmented but thorough. The predictions
of the psychologists, she said, were mechanistic, founded on the
mythos of cause-and-effect, or else on the-reality-as-given, and
omitted at their base the essential "unsurprise of surprise," which
sufficed not only for art, but even more for the human configuration. Here Brill jumped a little: it struck him that she had
somehow gotten her hands on Dr. Glypost's report; but this was
of course not possible; it was locked up in the safe of his private
office, where no one would ever have access to it, except now and
then a teacher coming to seek a clue to some deficiency, some
mystery of character. But no parent, never! And yet, when she
said "mechanistic," and "cause-and-effect," and all the rest, he
nearly quivered: it was as if she was accusing him, on account of
Dr. Glypost's prediction. It was *that* sort of prediction, she
declared—"the judgment from early performance"—that nour-
ished what (here she raised her head from the gray sheet) she was
then and there determined to call "the hoax of pedagogy."

Brill listened heavily now, concentrated in every grain, and so
did the rows and rows around him. He wondered if they were
teachers; or a collection of principals or school administrators; or
else a roomful of "epistemologists," like the silent furry men on
the platform. It troubled him that she was so derisive—or call it
ironic—but also it was evident enough that if she was ironic her

audience could not have been teachers or school bureaucrats. He decided they must all be philosophers, and when they laughed—again and again, and always at that word "hoax"—it was confirmed for him that they were. She heaped up analogies, allusions, hypotheses—she was frighteningly erudite. What awed him most were the strange links she wove between vivid hard circumstance and things that were only imagined. Her fables were curiously like certain paintings he was to see, and be broken by, in later years. It was her charm to quote from midrash, but though Brill wore his yarmulke always, and was, at least in this, indistinguishable from any Rosh Yeshiva, something in him— he thought it must be the astronomer—did not allow him to believe that midrash was *min hashamayim*, a species of celestial anecdote, a particle of the Oral Law, to be held equal with the Written. To him these little stories were only that: little stories made up to color a moral lesson; and when she began with "There ran the little fox," he knew at once which midrash it would be, and could not, for himself, see the connection with her subject.

T here ran the little fox," she said, "on the Temple Mount, in the place where the Holy of Holies used to be, barren and desolate, returned to the wild, in the generation of the Destruction. And Rabbi Akiva was walking by with three colleagues, Rabbi Gamliel, Rabbi Elazar, and Rabbi Joshua, and all four saw the little fox dash out. Three of the four wept, but Akiva laughed. Akiva asked, 'Why do you weep?' The three said, 'Because the fox goes in and out, and the place of the Temple is now the fox's place.' Then the three asked Akiva, 'Why do you laugh?' Akiva said, 'Because of the prophecy of Uriah and because of the prophecy of Zechariah. Uriah said, "Zion shall be ploughed as a field, and Jerusalem shall become heaps." Zechariah said, "Yet again shall the streets of Jerusalem be filled with boys and girls playing." So you see,' said Rabbi Akiva, 'now that Uriah's prophecy has been fulfilled, it is certain that Zechariah's prophecy will also be fulfilled.' And *that*," said Hester Lilt, "is pedagogy. To predict not from the first text, but from the second. Not from the earliest evidence, but from the latest. To laugh out loud in that very interval which to every reasonable judgment looks to be the most inappropriate—when the first is accomplished and future repair is most chimerical. To expect, to welcome, exactly that which appears most unpredictable. To await the surprise which, when it comes, turns out to be not a surprise after all, but a natural path." Again she lifted her head. "The hoax is when the pedagogue stops too soon. To stop at Uriah without the expectation of Zechariah is to stop too soon. And when the pedagogue stops too soon, he misreads every sign, and thinks the place of the priest is by rights the place of the fox, and takes the fox and all its qualities to be right, proper, and permanent; and takes aggressiveness for intelligence, and thoughtfulness for stupidity, and diffidence for dimness, and arrogance for popularity, and dreamers for blockheads, and brazenness for the mark of a lively personality. And all the while the aggressive and the brazen one is only a fox!—a false and crafty creature running in and out of a desolation and a delusion. The laughter of Akiva outfoxes the fox."

It was surely the most eccentric lecture on Theory of Education Principal Brill had ever heard. It was unlike her books—more fevered with parody, and then contorted beyond parody, so that once again it seemed wholly straightforward. In the light of this, he wondered about the cunning of her taste—he distrusted her. To seize on this midrash of the Destruction of the Temple, with all its melancholy at the gateway of Exile, and to miniaturize it into an emblem of teachers and pupils! She was daring, her pursuit was prodigal, she was afraid of nothing: and then, quite tamely, she arrived at the bee, she settled down with the bee: with the entelechy of the bee; how the bee, midflight, is the instrument of Purpose, though its fuzz and its buzz and its wingedness have knowledge only of their own freedom. And what did this have to do with pedagogy, this passenger bee joyful in its airy swoop downward upon the blossomy bed? It smells, it sees, it flies, all of its own will, all of its own delight, and all the while the poor gulled bee is a puppet, artfully deceived, deluded, managed and manipulated. Recondite to any human eye, the pigments in the plants and flowers reflect high-energy ultraviolet light, this invisible yet shouting shine lures on the sensitive bee, it lights in the belief it wills to light, when the truth is it is being drawn on by the paradisal fragrances of the secret sugar compounds that ambush it amid nectar and pollen. And the same with us: when we most imagine ourselves drunken and wild, en route to more wine or to our self-made whim, that is when we are most tethered; it is only that we have stopped too soon, before the playing-out of prophecy. And prophecy is penitential patience.

And so he took it all as accusation, after all—she had summoned him to squat there, a penitent, and again hear himself accused of having stopped too soon. She herself did not stop too soon: she exhausted every image of folly, exhausted the bee (whose habits, alone in the garden and in community in the hive, she minutely reviewed, until Brill felt himself in full possession of beedom), exhausted the evidence about the cannibal galaxies, those megalosaurian colonies of primordial gases that devour smaller brother-galaxies—and when the meal is made, the victim continues to rotate like a Jonah-dervish inside the cannibal, while the sated ogre-galaxy, its gaseous belly stretched, soporific, never spins at all—motionless as digesting Death. She exhausted even Akiva, about whom there were ten thousand tales (she did not omit his fanciful dictum on teachers, "More than the calf wishes to suck does the cow yearn to suckle"), she exhausted everything but the little ardent pack of her listeners. She led them all behind her as if on a spiral stair, new refreshment coming with each stunned turn upward toward the summit. At the summit, light like a noise—whereupon, with the abruptness of the finish, she sat down. What did he now understand that he had not understood before? That one must never stop too soon. Instantly the two bearded epistemologists undertook to "discuss," and only then did Brill begin to understand what he had understood. The pair were better groomed in learning than Gorchak, but they were Gorchak. Brill discovered himself again dampened by an ordinary pond, which was to say in the range of the commonplace: it was an impoverishment. They "discussed," they commented, they summarized, they followed, they flowed; the pond waters lapped and skipped, shallows of the Phlegethon!—they were hard workers of the mind, they had read much. But they spoke mainly in nouns, they were filled with pebbles of noun-endings: "-fication," "-ixation," "-ingness," "-terfusion," "-soplasm," "-ibility," "-ism," "-seosity," "-ization." They left out the bee, the little fox, the laughter of Akiva.

From all these—the bee, the little fox, the laughter of Akiva, especially the cannibal galaxy—Brill did not feel estranged. He suspected, in fact, that the lecturer's familiarity with the midrash was secondhand, and not out of the original text or tongue. As for the devouring galaxy, he was confident that she could not aspire to his own command of that affair: how Dr. François Schweizer and his colleagues had studied (via the 158-inch telescope at the Cerro Tololo Inter-American Observatory in Chile) the skies of the Southern Hemisphere, and how the name NGC 1316 fell to the one devourer whom they had examined in detail, owing to its emission of pronouncedly vigorous radio signals—a dusty swallower speckled by hundreds of billions of stars, its smaller prey being somewhat equivalent to one hundred million times the mass of our puny earthly sun. Nevertheless Brill could not have seen, on his own, how the pinwheel cosmos interprets pedagogy. For him the cosmos was always inhuman, of a terrible coldness, and far away, even though one lived in its midst. For her it was a long finger tapping.

T he next morning, at school, earnestly Principal Brill observed the philosopher's daughter. This time he did not enter the classroom but went behind the playground and up the stairs of the hayloft, to his own dim bed. From here, with the shade lifted (his bachelor's apartment had no curtains anywhere), and kneeling on the bed to give him the advantage of the window's aerie, he enjoyed as good a view of the first grade in recess as he could have had if they had all been marched past him one by one. The first-graders were swinging on the swings and clambering in and out of the jungle gym: the soles of small shoes and white socks crammed into them flashed by, high birdcries whinnied past. Two figures were separated from this scene, which had repeated itself every day, for years and years: the infinity of the little ones! It was true Brill had never before hidden himself in this way to look on, but had only taken it all in from the road; and from the road behind the playground the children seemed like colorful starlings, shrill and hopping under the elderly trees. One of the figures some distance apart from the others, the larger of the two, was Mrs. Bloomfield, who sat on a faraway rock with her dangling dark hair swaying over the shiny pages of a magazine. The playground supplied her with as much tedium as the classroom, but here she yielded herself license to withdraw. All the teachers were like this—would snatch at any consecutive row of minutes to close themselves off from obligation. Mediocrities.

Sluggards. Only Gorchak was unremittingly alert, like a fowl without eyelids. The second figure removed from the rest was Hester Lilt's child. Brill was not surprised by this. She had not altogether abandoned the center of play, but only stood there in her pale dress and watched the others. The sun threw a kind of powdery satin over her hair, which was smoothly divided into two round bronze curls, fallen on either side of her collar. Her knees were pressed tightly together, and her fingers were entwined in the lifted hem of her dress, twisting. Otherwise she did not stir; she was an onlooker. When someone did a trick and all the others squalled their laughter—on the topmost bar a boy hanging upside down from his heels, that negligent fool Bloomfield!—there passed over Beulah Lilt's eyes and cheeks a tentative, almost a fearful, glimmer, what Brill's oldest sister Claire would have called a *shmeykhele*, the wraith of an amusement toyed with inside a desolation of solitude. Long afterward, when he remembered the moment, he thought perhaps she had been pleased by some curious pattern: the dangling boy's legs crisscrossed over the crisscross of the bars, and all the small leaves of bushes quivering in masses behind. Except for this diffident near-smile, afraid of itself, Brill could not read anything at all in her face, as oval and thin as an antique coin. He only marked it out that while the others tumbled about like a yardful of geese, flailing and elbowing and crowing and crowding, the philosopher's daughter was perfectly friendless. It was not that the turbulence avoided her, but rather that she was not noticed by it. If she had been anyone else's daughter, Brill would not have pitied her; even now he did not pity her. But he was disappointed all over again. He had come with a stony purpose: to scrutinize the child of Hester Lilt. He meant to unravel, to decode, the mother. Somewhere in the child the amazing mother lurked. The children always contained the mothers; he knew this to be true without exception, having fixed his eye a thousand times on the shape of a thumbnail familiar because of the mother's thumbnail, or the recurrence of an insignificant gesture, even something so minute as a millimeter's elevation of a shoulder muscle. It was all there always, nature's prank of duplication: in the skin, in the shin, in the position of an ear in relation to a hairline, in the arc of a lip; and even more than that, in a jeer, in a word, in a lie; especially in forwardness; especially in assertiveness. The shy begat the shy (though few were shy), the combative begat the combative.

Principal Brill kneeled on his bed and peered down into the playground, and saw nothing of the strange mother in the strange child.

B y the second grade Beulah Lilt had of course learned to read. On the other side of the Curriculum— the Scriptural side—she was weak. She was weak also in arithmetic. She was weak in "class participation": she never raised her hand to offer an answer. It was assumed she did not know the answer. Sometimes she did know it; sometimes she did not. Already the class had grown into the configuration it was to keep term after term: already it could be seen which would be Gorchak's favorites. Gorchak had favorites. Seelenhohl had favorites as well, but whereas Gorchak's favorites were those who had the highest marks, slothful Seelenhohl liked best those who were loudest and longest in "class participation." She esteemed the glib, and rewarded four-flushers by encouraging the exercise of what she called "student opinion," "independent analysis," "democratic airing of issues"— her real aim was to fill the hour without having to prepare for it. Brill knew Seelenhohl was a cheat and an idler, yet she was one of the few besides Gorchak who could keep absolute order. There was no yowling and no chaos in her room; she was a secret terrorist. Brill never learned what the instruments of her tyranny were. When he opened her door he was impressed by the calm. It was only that something tentative in the rows of faces suggested intimidation; the children were afraid of Mrs. Seelenhohl. How did she threaten them, with what? Was it her voice, some ugliness in her look? She had a long crocodile smile: she was all teeth from ear to ear, but there she stood, in her nice dress and her stockings and her pumps, smiling widely with her pretty face, and who could be afraid of that? The aisles between the chairs were tidy. There was no noise, only the empty exposition of a "student opinion," winding and winding, like elongated spittle.

Brill did not again ask Hester Lilt to address the parent body. She did not again ask him to a public talk. Her talks were infrequent, in any case. He kept himself informed—he watched over whatever came from her lips or her pen. The heat, the mazy network of enigma, the conflagration of Hester Lilt's mind! She was a sorcerer. A sorcerer cannot beget a sorcerer; the law of reproduction had failed for the philosopher's daughter. By the fourth grade he took it for granted that Dr. Glypost's prediction would hold. Beulah was an undistinguished child, and worse: it was as if she suffered from an unremitting bewilderment. She sat like a deaf-mute. When the others ran she stood stiffly at the periphery. The teachers thought her dull. And meanwhile there were all the lively ones—how many answers they had, what wit, what a blaze of child-acuity the lively bright ones flaunted! It was Principal Brill's trick to break without warning into a classroom and pounce on the clever children with mathematical riddles; or else he would seize a stick of chalk and splash on the blackboard, in what the teachers called his "European" script, a fragment of the fable from *Aphrodite*:

He liked to roam in the moonlight through the peaceful glades, holding in his hand a little tortoise shell in which were fastened two aurochs horns strung with three silver strings. When his fingers touched the strings, a delightful music would sound, sweeter far than the babble of the streams or the whisper of the wind in the trees or in the grain. The first time he played, three couched tigers sat up, so prodigiously charmed that they offered him no ill but came as near as they could and then withdrew when he had ceased playing. The next day, there were many more of them, and there were wolves, and hyenas, and snakes poised upright

—though he heard how they tittered and mocked the lines when the door shut behind him. Long ago, Claude had made him memorize the whole passage: it was about Orpheus. He stood outside the classroom and looked down at his chalk-whitened right hand; an Orphic melancholy pierced him. He longed for a noble scholarship—the pleasure-pain of poetry and the comely orderliness of number and the logical passion of Gemara, all laced together in an illustrious tapestry; but he had only these children, the cleverest not clever enough, the mothers shallow brass, the fathers no more than plumbers, the teachers vessels of philistinism, rude, crude, uncultivated, unbookish, raw, oh the ignorance, the vulgarity! Middling, middling! Himself the governor of all this. Royal charlatan.

And she, Hester Lilt, a presence in that place though never present: a specter of sorts. The myriad meetings of the mothers' groups—fund-raisers, they fashioned paper flowers; organized bazaars, lotteries, all the kitsch of their coffee and cake, hairdos, exercise classes, tennis camps, and oh God the rest of it, Gothic novels, "gourmet" recipes, cards, trivia, the one or two who aspired to write "juveniles"—he took it for granted that she never went near any of it. Doubtless the mothers—seeing in her only what the eye afforded—despised her for her aloofness. A Brahmin among untouchables, red-stained in her brow's precise center. In her apartness Brill caught the scarlet flare of his own bright dream: serenity, absorption, civilization, intellect, imagination. Soaring. It was as if someone had set on him, for the second time (Claude was the first), a sacred stain. For a few months following that distant unforgotten talk (the laughter of Akiva, he privately named it), he dangled on the rim of infatuation after all; then pulled back. Safe. Again he had stopped too soon, but was glad of it: he had his wits still. She engrossed him, she engaged him, she drew him. No longer diffident, he sought the telephone often, and it was curious that she was almost always there, accessible to his wish, and willing enough to bend toward him for ten minutes at a time. He reflected that, on her side, it was the obligation of the bargain she had struck; it must be for the sake of the child. But he could do nothing for her child. He could not. He saw the fourth grade flash by, then the fifth, the sixth, the years frantically counted in grades, and all these flashings, these passings, were his tragedy, because it was not given to him to chase time through to its disclosures. If Beulah left the sixth grade, the sixth grade was still there, altered not at all; the sixth grade and all the other grades were all he had; the sixth grade never vanished, though one day Beulah would; however many children vanished, time would not move; there was again a sixth grade, and would be into eternity, and he, who could not abolish the timelessness of all this, felt the thoroughness, the repletion, of the curse of perpetuity. Hydra-headed replenishment, Keats's urn, but overflowing.

No form grows old in such a hell.

In the seventh grade something minutely changed. Beulah appeared now to be a member of a pack. Brill had only blurred inklings of the society of the girl-pack. He observed that it had a leader, and that the others went where led. The pack darted from classroom to corridor, whooping. The leader was one of the clever girls, chief among Gorchak's current favorites, the daughter of a fearless mother good at argument. The child was the mother's seedling precisely, and already had the habit of power; she directed who would run with her and who would stay behind. She was witty and able and cocky and quick, everything that Gorchak most admired, and since she was also slender-waisted and tall—not as a child is tall, but as a woman is—Gorchak looked at her with a lover's eye. She was his little classroom wife, the first to join him in mocking the weak pupils. And when, fingering Chumash, Gorchak came to the Hebrew word for concubine, *pilegesh*, the class felt it already knew what this meant: there she sat, in a middle row, Gorchak's *pilegesh*, the dark and dazzling one, with the highest marks and all her fawning attendants. Seelenhohl said to Gorchak, in Brill's hearing, "Odd that Beulah's in with Corinna"—Corinna was the vivid leader—"because usually the smart ones don't travel with the dimwits"; but Gorchak said, "They don't accept her, she runs after them." They were absorbed by the politics of the children's lives: who was high and powerful, who inferior and humiliated, whose stock was rising, whose going down. They were drawn to the power of the leader as if they themselves belonged to the society of the pack; they were consumed by it. It meant nothing to them, Brill saw, that Beulah's mother was Hester Lilt.

Gorchak and Seelenhohl ministered only to the upper school—they taught the seventh and eighth grades—and Beulah was now in their hands: in the hands of Gorchak, who wanted only right answers exactly memorized; in the hands of Seelenhohl, who wanted no answers at all, only tactics and guesswork. Seelenhohl's "subject" was Social Studies—i.e., history, but what was that, what did she imagine history to be? She told Brill she was "training their minds," she with her spread-out crocodile grin and her neat shoes and her democratic airings and her secret tyranny! One of the mothers—not surprisingly, it was Mrs. Dorothea Luchs, Corinna's combative mother—came roaring to Principal Brill that Mrs. Seelenhohl had given a test and recorded everyone's mark—

and that Corinna, leading her pack, had opened Mrs. Seelenhohl's desk drawer one afternoon and found the pile of tests, not
one of them even looked at. On the day before report cards, Brill
composed a memo:

Dear Mrs. Seelenhohl:

It has come to my attention that your midterm examination, on
the Roman Empire, was observed by several pupils to be lying in
your desk ungraded. Though you had not yet evaluated these papers,
yet it is evident you were somehow able to intuit what each was
worth, since this office is already in receipt of your midterm grades.
I assume you invented these rather than take the time to read each
child's examination. Of course, it is always a teacher's prerogative
to decide what will and what won't "count," what will and what
won't enter into her judgment of a child's performance and progress.
But an ungraded and unreturned test is, morally and pedagogically,
worse than no test at all. It teaches what no good or bad mark on
a test can teach—i.e., that sometimes the adult world does not
mean what it says, that sometimes an adult promise can be broken,
that effort will not always bring reward, that reputation is immuta-
ble and cannot be ameliorated by reform, that restitution is impossible, etc., etc. Such an incident encourages in children an attitude
of fatalism (contrary to our religious teachings) as well as resigna-
tion and hopelessness.

In my view the issue is not that you arbitrarily filled in the marks
(your guesses may very well have come quite close), but that the
children believed that the test was given in good faith and that,
whether or not the teacher *meant* it to "count," the children,
discovering that it did not, experienced a breach of trust. Pupils
need to have confidence in the meticulous attention of teachers—
again, attention not to marks, but to the instillation of trust. Otherwise the world will be perceived chiefly as an arena for betrayal. It
is difficult enough to practice the moral life under any conditions,
and the larger world is, clearly, sometimes an arena for betrayal.
But shouldn't we in the teaching profession, we who are called to

the Socratic and prophetic vocation, shouldn't *we*, at least, be relied on not to be an arena for early betrayal?

If I hear of this happening again, I would hope that you would find it convenient to look for employment elsewhere next year.

> Faithfully,
> J. Brill
> Principal, Edmond Fleg School

He was proud of this letter. How well-written it was! It took him a whole night. It made him feel restored, enlarged; it was as if he had ennobled himself by fitting together, shard by shard, an almost-forgotten palace. Once he had known himself to be just such an honorable soul, a man of faith and sincerity buried in a dungeon in Egypt, with just such a gift for the phraseology of idealism. "Pupils need to have confidence in the meticulous attention of teachers—again, attention not to marks, but to the instillation of trust." While he was writing this sentence, and just as the long dash made its stripe, his vital organs seemed to swell inside their envelope of red flesh, and it was as if he stood in the after-school muteness and greenness, leaning his breast toward the road.

He composed a second memo; but this one was only imaginary. It danced in his head enticingly:

Dear Mrs. Dorothea Luchs:

Your daughter, though tall and pretty, is a sneak and a potential destroyer of the lives of young and old. Her act of snooping inside Mrs. Seelenhohl's desk almost forces me to jeopardize the employment of an otherwise satisfactory teacher, who is no more incompetent than any of the others, and in matters of reliability rather more desirable than the average female teacher. Moreover, I have been watching your daughter. She acquires her so-called "popularity" through exclusion. She blesses those whom she blesses. The rest she discards. I believe this is what they term a "clique." Your daughter has turned the Lilt child into a tail. In addition, it may be that your daughter's high grades are based on pushiness and the inability of ignorant teachers to discriminate between the priest and the fox.

In the end he did not send the real memo either. He was afraid Seelenhohl, offended, *would* look for employment elsewhere, and then what would he do? Where would he find another Social Studies teacher who, at a frugal salary, would have so fine an attendance record combined with the stern capacity to keep order?

On Beulah Lilt's report card Seelenhohl wrote: "Beulah is a quiet child who should try harder." Gorchak wrote coldly, "Beulah looks out of the window too much. Therefore you must expect her to remain in the lowest quarter of the class."

The report card was returned with Hester Lilt's mannish signature. The "Parents' Comments" space was blank. By now Brill no longer anticipated anything else. It was as if she had vowed to pretend she had no child. She was not maternal. The other mothers, meanwhile, on the day after report cards, drove into the school's graveled lot in a fury, brandishing sheaves of old tests, counting up points, demanding changes, shouting reminders of illnesses and days absent, excusing and denouncing: Mrs. Bloomfield in tears, Gorchak's thrust-out chin a rosy stone axe, exposing in all that hardness an unexpected tic, Seelenhohl snapping her teeth with a steely ring, the Principal himself besieged in his dark office. On one wall hung a trio of sages: Spinoza, Einstein, Freud. All three looked deeply lethargic—Freud gazed down at his shoelaces, one of which had come untied and lay loose on the floor like a worm. Only Miss Fifferling, the third-grade teacher, raised her soldierly neck and shrieked back at the phalanx of mothers.

Hester Lilt did not make an appearance on this day or on any other. She kept away. Was she indifferent to her own child? Did she not understand that Beulah was in disgrace, that Beulah was hopeless, that Beulah was a cause for shame? Brill fancied himself in unnerved possession of an infinitely sad secret: the daughter was not equal to the mother. He wondered whether the mother knew this; and yet how could she not know it? And knowing it, how could she not grieve? He telephoned her; he intended to talk about Beulah's report card. But she would not give in. She would not say Beulah's name. If he spoke of the stars, she was ready for him; if he spoke of the universe, or of his sisters, or of winter nights in the Paris of his boyhood, or of his father, his mother, of his old teachers (whether Pult or Gaillard), of certain translations, of pedagogy; if he brought up some aspect of Gemara, some bright narrow unexplored cranny—how heedful she was then, how amenable to hearing him out! Only he must not speak of Beulah. When he began about Beulah—how Gorchak, for instance, deplored her muteness, how Seelenhohl never thought of her at all—she would lead him into another kind of telling. He told her what he had never expected to tell: how Rabbi Pult had once beckoned Gabriel and Loup close to his chair among the brown-glass brine bottles (though in the telling he omitted the bottles and the back room of the *poissonnerie*) and said, in their small brother's hearing, "Always negate. Negate, negate"; and how he, young as he was, was horrified, because he believed Rabbi Pult was purposing to distort his brothers by drawing them, old as *they* were, from the society of the normal. "They were big boys then, into their teens," he explained.

"And you?" Hester Lilt asked.

"A little chap."

"And were you thinking even then about what is normal and what is not? Even then?"

"I always think of the abnormal," he said. "It's a form of self-regard."

It was the faintest sort of sally, but she brushed it away. "What did he mean by that—Pult, your Rabbi Pult?"

A catechism. How he liked, with her, the chance to be free with his Latin! "*Odi profanum vulgus.* He meant that."

"Did he really?" She considered. "Only to keep away from what the crowd likes? Didn't he mean anything less frivolous than that?"

A Rabbi Pult who was not serious enough—*there* was a picture! "No, no," he urged, "it was a way of telling them to take for granted that most people are trivial."

"Most people are trivial?"

"Yes," he said, under the pressure of her repetition; again he felt her parody.

"What became of him?"

"Rabbi Pult?"

"Pult."

"He disappeared."

"And your brothers?"

"Disappeared."

"Then it was the wrong evaluation, wasn't it? If most people are trivial, they wouldn't haul off other people. They'd spend their lives going to the museum instead."

This seemed so callous and hard that he did not know what to make of her. And "museum"!—as if she knew to mock his roundabout way, though, among all his boyhood tellings, he had never told her this. Her head the head, on its stout neck, of de Sévigné; but only that once, and never again. Still, he felt her implicated in the roundabout way, and what it led to; she was a European, like himself. In one moment she had disposed of Pult: his hallowed teacher of blessed memory. Yet she too negated. She more than anyone negated. She above all. "Isn't that just what *you* do?" he said. "You turn the habitual inside out. You look for the unexpected in everything. You negate."

"I negate nothing," she said. "I never put myself in contradiction with myself."

It was clear he would get no more from her just then. He had skimmed close to his hidden life—told about Pult, told about Gabriel and Loup. His losses. Between them there ought to have been the bond of the ravished. Europe the cannibal galaxy. Edmond Fleg's Parisian Jerusalem a smoky ruin. He saw how France was Egypt. But she was finished. She had yielded him his usual ten minutes, moving off now to return to—what? She appeared to be always at home, unlike the mothers who ran here and there. A waterfall of books, the hunch of her female shoulders. He tried to imagine Hester Lilt standing, as other women did, at a kitchen counter preparing supper for Beulah. Or watching at the window for the school bus. Or leaning down over her child's head to look at the homework. All these commonplace postures failed. It was as if she had escaped her body and the fruit of her body. It was as if she lived without anecdote; as if nothing had ever happened to her. Only mind. She was free of event because she was in thrall to idea. Yet the child was *there*, had been born, in the regular way, out of the fork of a woman. Despite everything she was in contradiction with herself: she had given birth to her opposite. An opposite is an opponent; perhaps she hated the child, was sickened by her blankness, abased by her insipidness—or did she never think of the child at all? Yet the child was fed, dressed, attended to. Did the philosopher ever talk to her daughter? He wished he could eavesdrop at bedtime.

Instead, he called Beulah to his office. His motives were the same as before: sly. But now he was not searching for the mother in the daughter; it was the daughter herself he was after. He had learned nothing from the playground. If he again invaded the classroom it would be useless: Beulah would not lift her eyes. Even now, hands hiding, little straight rods of legs taking turns at scraping back, she kept her head down, so that the line of the hair-part peered up at him like a white mouth shut tight against his inquisition.

"I've asked you here, Beulah, to become acquainted."

Silence.

"After all, your mother and I are such good friends. We have had so many interesting conversations about so many interesting subjects. I don't have to tell you about your mother—"

Silence like an interruption. She raised her chin and her eyes rolled up like green stones. He tried to read them, but could not. She was impregnable. He could not blame the teachers for impatience with such a pair of stony eyes.

"You must be so proud of your mother, and there are so many remarkable things she must teach you. There are, you know, so many remarkable things she's taught *me*. Your mother is a whole school, what do you think of that?"

Again the dropped head, the white mute line slashed through it.

He was determined to provoke. "I notice you're friends with Corinna Luchs. We're all so proud of Corinna. At Commencement next year she may very well be valedictorian. Mr. Gorchak thinks so, at any rate. It wouldn't surprise me in the least, though she's running neck and neck with Becky Gould. Those are both very bright students, and their mothers are very hard workers in the P.T.A. We'd be lost without Mrs. Luchs—she gets all the other mothers to work, and the last raffle brought in eight hundred dollars. That was all Corinna's mother's doing, the costume tea was her idea." He ended, "You like Corinna, don't you?"

The smallest shrug.

Oh, the absence of language, how could it be? If, unlike the others, she had no jabber, how could it be that she had no language? He got up from the Bristol chair (its upturned wooden hand seemed just then appalling, a deranged artisan's mad thought) and went to the other side of the desk and took her stiff wrist and led her to the photograph of Freud, nervous over his untied shoe, the great black mirror-eyes of Spinoza, Einstein as detached as some Hindu holy man.

"Do you know who these men in the pictures are, Beulah?"

She kept him waiting with her silent head.

"Men," he said, "who were never in contradiction with themselves. Do you know what that means? I'm not sure I do, either.

Ask your mother—it's something *she* said. But I can tell you that these very intelligent men never stopped too soon. They went as far as their brains would take them, and their brains took them very far. Do you know what a genius is, Beulah?"

She rolled up her two green stones, and he threw his words against them. "It's what neither you nor I can ever be. You are not a genius, and neither am I. Do you and your mother have many talks?"

"Sometimes"—very low.

"And what are they about?"

The shrug. "Things."

He sent her back to the classroom then. A futility. He had hoped to refute Bloomfield and Dr. Glypost and Seelenhohl and Gorchak, to penetrate the drowning ship's hold and discover the kidnapped babe.

In the afternoon, a wide tumult: Corinna Luchs leading her pack; Beulah flying anxiously after.

H e relinquished the philosopher's daughter. He let his curiosity halt; he abandoned it. He had taken too much trouble—Beulah was not the first dim pupil in his school. She would not be the last. His school was not the children's Sorbonne; it was only, despite Dual Curriculum, mediocre American. America the vulgar. Its children had no language. Each spring, at Commencement, he said *ad astra*; he said *ad astra* to the mothers. He used Abélard's Latin to tell lies with, because time shudders and uncovers perpetuity. Mornings, running to the beach, he felt his schoolmaster's grief. He was sick of nature's pledge: daughters becoming mothers, the amaranthine first grade, the eighth grade unfailingly pubescent—Beulah, though her legs were still unrounded rods, was beginning breasts. She passed into the eighth grade without his noticing. He let her slip. She was submerged; he was no longer aware. He thought of Hester Lilt but not of Beulah Lilt. He cut the child from the mother; it was no more than the mother herself had done. On the beach of the Phlegethon, seeing each new wave identically supplant the previous wave, it came to him one freezing dawn that he was dying of unchangingness; he was dying of lack of death—his reason was deprived, he was like a barbarian who cannot fathom the link between copulation and procreation. He could not dream the end, no one grew old for him.

The washed sand was a snowfall. Quickly the heels of his sneakers were sucked down and buried. The waves were white, like snowy beards shearing themselves. The white dawn hesitated behind all that sharper whiteness. In the cold, sunk in that snow-sand pocked by those primeval shells (the life in them cleaned out, scooped, eaten, decomposed, the shell-walls polished, pearly, snow white), he decided to marry.

It was the hiring season. The new young teachers streamed into his office, and he sorted them out: this one too arrogant, that one in danger of becoming pregnant too soon. He asked few questions and did not impede their chatter. They opened out their palms and sermonized on the education of children while he handled their papers. In every dossier he saw stupidity; in their faces stupidity was peculiarly combined with vivacity. What they were in reality was a species of low theater folk, vaudevillians, and in addition to this strain of the histrionic they harbored an inclination to dominate and to crush. The young women often spoke of love; they loved children, they wanted to "work with" children, and in this, he saw, lay the peril: they did not love learning or work. They did not love verbs. They did not love the confluence of like or unlike numbers. They did not love maps. (Pult: *With the love of learning comes the love of whoever learns. In the absence of the love of learning there can be only self-love.*) He hired the most vivacious; they made the best impression on the parents, even though they were also the most marriageable. Still, there was the case of Dina Fifferling, excellent at discipline. From her classroom, as from Seelenhohl's, no noise issued. Instead he heard the plainsong of Miss Fifferling's long, long vocabulary lists. Miss Fifferling dealt with the third grade as if they were hostile infiltrators. She feared sabotage. She had a brave chin, an admirable oval nose, and quick lynx lids; she was altogether pert; her hair was electrically rectilinear, like a sheet of negative particles. Brill believed she would surely be engaged before the school year was out. Unexpectedly she fell into a reliable spinsterhood. She developed a scowl and he did not lose her. He suspected her of heartlessness, but the mothers failed to complain. One practice he was certain of: she read aloud the names of those who had the lowest marks, and this somehow cowed the mothers of the weak pupils. She had regularly read aloud Beulah Lilt's marks. But Mrs. Dorothea Luchs went out of her way to praise Miss Fifferling: Corinna was the only child Miss Fifferling—in ten years of teaching—had ever kissed.

Brill hired four new teachers, all young women. There was a young man he was tempted by, a sweet-voiced yeshiva student, but then he thought better of it: this boy with his soft camel-eyes would soon become the head of a family, have mouths to feed, his voice would sour, he would demand too much money. Meanwhile there was an office crisis: the clerk-receptionist quarreled with one of the secretaries and quit. Routinely Brill took on a new clerk-receptionist, and this was almost a pleasure. It was straightforward and clean. He liked the idea of a clerk-receptionist: the odd humble hierarchical stammer of it, the modest linking hyphen, the plain pure sound of sorting-out, the promise of bustle and orderliness. There was no torment in any of it. He gave the job to a twenty-nine-year-old young woman with an elderly bun, black and shining as fresh tar, and blue-black ink-moist bangs, a divorcée who lived alone with her child, a boy six years old. She seemed unreasonably tall, taller than any of the secretaries, taller than the teachers, taller than himself, and this appealed to him. He was drawn to heights of every kind.

On the telephone he continued to ply Hester Lilt with anecdotes. He assailed her, he was persistent. The instrument relieved him. The blindness of these conversations had the effect of a confessor's screen: he felt himself both hidden and exposed. Of her appearance he recalled mainly the white splash of hair, the infrequent bailiff's smile, more suspicious than not. She pried open his anecdotes for their consequences. Every image, she said, has its logic: every story, every tale, every metaphor, every mood, is inhabited by a language of just deserts. We judge a myth by its practical influences, and are obliged to ask it practical questions: What do you intend? Who should respect you? What will you cause? What do you disclose about envy, cruelty, lust, hope, growth, power, choice, faith, pity? Whose mouth should receive you? (Pult: *Why is it that the stork, a loving parent, is shunned as impure?*) On his side he still did not know the simplest datum of her life—was she someone's wife? Then whose? Fish after the grain of language, she instructed him, look for the idiom in the wilderness of a narrative; distrust poetry. He already did. In reality the heavens are gases and express physics. He told her that when he was a young man—he was still in the earliest stages of his study of vapors—he had once prayed very deeply. The liturgy that afternoon penetrated the secret channels of his brain; he understood his mouth's work for the first time, even though he had chanted those same words every day from boyhood, and they were as familiar to him as his own bedclothes. These domesticated and intimate syllables had all at once taken on an enchantment, an illumination. He was stunned by what he heard in them. He left the prayer hall exulting, strange even to himself. As soon as he crossed the threshold someone spoke to him, a fellow student. Brill rebuffed him. He was sharp; he was coiled and cold in his own strangeness. The rabbi—it was Pult—came out and summoned him back. "Joseph," Pult said, "come here and daven. You have not davened." Brill protested, "Rabbi, I just finished davening. You saw me. You heard me." Pult said: "If you pray and then you go out and embarrass someone, you have not prayed."

All that was on the afternoon of the day Claude had called him Dreyfus.

On the far side of the wire he heard nothing. Then Hester Lilt said loudly, "You've never visited us. Why not?"

So he went. It was an ordinary Tuesday evening, and he was elated; everything pleased him. He was used to the new flat houses and false-brick fences and new dwarfish trees of the "developments" inhabited by all the others. He liked it that she lived in a modest apartment building in the center of one of the nearby towns; he was himself an urban soul. Hester Lilt was quartered in three European rooms. There were fewer books than he had fancied—uneven heaps, not very high, on plain tables. The furniture was old. Nothing glinted—there was no metal—and what seemed European was not so much what was all around as what was missing. A scarred piano, but no other source of music, none of the appliances of sound. All the same, he walked into an uproar. He saw the telephone almost immediately: an important figurine, black baal, his access and tunnel to her, docile now and displaced in this last-century cranny. It mesmerized him. It was a pair of headless shoulders, surrounded by photographs, all of the same young man, mustached, broad-nostriled. He did not dare to ask whether this was her husband. "My father. Long ago," she said. He knew she would never tell about her father, her husband, her life. What a din! He followed her through mysterious school-noise to wherever she led.

It was a children's party. Paper peaked hats, balloons, yellow donkey-tails, a paper tablecloth with a red-buttoned Mickey Mouse in the middle. Fat pink cake mostly eaten, dead candles sprawled. She had achieved the American thing exactly: the thing most middling. He recognized Corinna Luchs and her pack. They shrieked wildly when he entered—it was a bedroom, the bed with a big board on it, converted to a dining table. "Principal Brill! Principal Brill!" he heard, but he was transfixed: he was looking at the philosopher's bed.

"You are our coup," she said.

"Principal Brill! Principal Brill!"

Briefly he succumbed to the pack—laughed, was jostled, felt himself entrapped, let them tease out his little jokes; then made his escape. But he was bitter. She had drawn him into mediocrity, she had nailed him into his usual place. Seeking her, he arrived at his pupils. He found the door and pulled on his driving-gloves and stood there: "You know I'm not always Principal Brill. Not every moment of life."

Hester Lilt said, "You are."

"Sometimes I'm Joseph Brill."

"And Joseph Brill is the Principal." Extraordinary: she who habitually denied him his title was just now cramming it down his craw.

He said angrily, "Not every moment."

"It's Beulah's *birthday.*"

This astonished him; from someone else he would have taken it to be a mother's cry. How many birthdays, with what flattery and strategy, had they cajoled him to, year after year! In the beginning he went if he thought he could get a contribution to the school out of it. Latterly he never went at all; he husbanded his luster, they vied for him.

"I don't go to parties for the children. I make no exceptions. If I went to every party I would be doing nothing else." And he himself understood that he sounded, precisely then, like someone who is always Principal Brill. From all the signs—whoops and frenzy—it might have been Corinna Luchs's birthday, or, failing that, Becky Gould's. They were running now, in and out among the little book-tables. Corinna was the leader. Beulah was the tail. Beulah at home was no different from Beulah at school. Was she innocent—the mother? Was she innocent of being who she was? Did she imagine he could have come for Beulah's sake? In the dim little vestibule, his gloved hand already on the doorknob, he calculated how to frame it.

He said: "I'm as helpless over Beulah as you are."

"Helpless?"

The echo made him coarse. "The father. She might be like her father. Is her father—" He sliced off the rest. He did not know what word to use. Lost? Mute? Eyes of dead stone?

Mildly, innocently, she said, "You want to hear things."

"I want," he began, still coarse; but then he did not know what it was he could want from her. He had tried to read *Metaphor as Exegesis*, assimilating not much of it; he had heard her speak of the fox, the bees, the cannibal galaxies. What more could he want from her?

To be free of this child. Never to have borne this child.

She was giving him a convoluted European story. It was her first telling; it depressed him. Even while she was yielding him a name, a fate, Brill withdrew the bloodhounds. He withdrew them. He could not take in what name and what fate—her husband was alive, or distant, or again married; in London or Antwerp or Lisbon or Leningrad; or back of the kitchen door; a thinker, a broom-maker, a wizard, a messenger—whether of diplomatic pouches or of some celestial novelty he could not tell; her father was a torrent, her mother a storm, her husband a silence or quicksilver lake. Or she had no husband at all. He thought of

Lot's daughters, lying down with their father in the destruction of the world in order to save the future. The face at the telephone was surely the father of her daughter. Or not. The more she delivered, the more she withheld. She meant him to seize everything and nothing. She knew herself to be a flake of history, someone destroyed, finished; old, the way the world after its destruction is old; whatever had once mattered did not matter now. She was all future; she cut the thread of genesis. Only Beulah mattered. Only Beulah. So he saw his deep mistake: it was not that she was not maternal. She was nothing else. It was her passion. *Amor intellectualis*—with the others it was reflex, instinct, involuntary pulse and impulse, the chorus of flesh in relentless repetition. But Hester Lilt's daughter was not for supplanting Hester Lilt; she was the philosopher's mystical salvation. He could not bear thinking this. In the end she would have no use for his Dual Curriculum, his two civilizations, his radiant antiquity. She would snuff out whatever happens, she would remove Beulah from any remnant of history. She would wipe her brain clean: the child would be fatherless and motherless. An orphan of the future. While the little girls ran whooping, Brill felt himself inwardly collapse. He was without urgency or interest now, it made no difference, he had no need for her to go on stripping and peeling herself. Shaming: he was embarrassed for her. He wished she would stop.

He broke in: "Consider yourself."

"Myself?"

"She's nothing."

"Nothing?" she said in surprise. "Who is nothing?"

The tail of the pack; the philosopher's daughter. "Beulah," he said, "isn't you."

"She's everything. She's my life."

"But you haven't any illusions," he said hollowly; now he knew better. "You can *see*."

"I can see that she's my life."

"Tigress and cublet, what rubbish! Mrs. Lilt," he pressed, "consider what you are, consider the differences—"

"There are no differences."

He said again, "Your child is not you."

"You don't know about Beulah. You don't know anything about Beulah. There aren't any differences between—between—" and he marveled to hear her nearly stutter, all her fingers spread out, slight short fingers with translucent low webs fanning out from the back of the hand. She did not finish. "You think I'm not like any of the mothers. You never say it, but I know what you think. I'm exactly like them, why shouldn't I be?"

He tried to maneuver around this. "You've made no claim, never. None on the school, none on me—never on me—none on the teachers. You've never taken any notice. Sometimes," he said, "a school is helpless. The teachers are helpless. I," he said, "am helpless."

"You don't know her."

"By now we ought to. We've had her for almost the whole of eight years." He moved from the door and leaned close to her. This way his "we" seemed less official. Her eyes were small and undistinguished. There was a white wart beneath one of them, caught in a bluish well. But he saw her terrifying intelligence.

"It's you who don't know her," he told her.

H e drove back to school—to his cramped ostler's rooms overlooking the playground. It seemed to him the little white wart under her eye was still glimmering. She was illusioned. She was not normal. Did she really suppose she was like all the rest of them—the mothers? Or did she posit Beulah as a higher idea that could be willed into being? The next morning he summoned the sweet-voiced yeshiva student and gave him a job. "A shift in plans," he told Gorchak. "You're too burdened, you need a respite. Take the third grade from Fifferling." Gorchak was agitated, his ruddy jowl twitched, his bush of red brambles shook: "The third grade? The third grade? What about Fifferling?" "I'm getting rid of her." "A month into the term?" "I don't want cruelty here, I won't have it." "The third grade," Gorchak spat out; up came his stone-axe chin, pink as rhubarb. "It's not a demotion, Ephraim, don't misunderstand. Someone has to get hold of the third grade. It's a shambles." "It's Seelenhohl who's the shambles," Gorchak said, "she doesn't teach them anything. Fifferling is all right. She keeps order." "She deals in public shame." "So do I," Gorchak said; "it makes them work. There's no reason on earth I'll take the third grade, I won't do it." "You will," Principal Brill said, and handed over the eighth grade to the sweet-voiced yeshiva student.

Instantly there appeared before Brill's desk Mrs. Dorothea Luchs, Mrs. Edith Horwich, Mrs. Lenore Billiger, Mrs. Phyllis Kramer, Mrs. Vanessa Lichtenberg, Mrs. Lillian Lebow.

"We are a committee," Mrs. Dorothea Luchs said, "on behalf of giving the eighth grade back to Mr. Gorchak. That was a rotten thing to do."

"Rabbi Sheskin is very able," Brill said.

"He's not even a rabbi yet. We don't know anything about him. He's a baby."

"He's only a few months away from ordination," Brill said. "He'll do." But he feared these women.

"He will *not* do," said Mrs. Dorothea Luchs. "Corinna *likes* Mr. Gorchak. They all like him."

The delegation collectively nodded: so many well-tended hairdos, up and down. Intruders. Would-be gynecocracy. He feared them, he intended to drive them away with a puff. On the wall behind him Principal Brill felt the severe stare of genius, his three hanged men. He had yoked them there like suns, to warm his back. Freud, Spinoza, Einstein. The mind, the universe, the abyss between. It came to him that he lived in the abyss. He was nothing beside these sages. As he was to them, so these women were to him. He saw himself the grub on Freud's shoe.

"You can't just turn things inside out right smack in the middle of the term," Mrs. Dorothea Luchs called, as from a long way off, though she stood there, straight as a cat, just in front of him, fixed on the wooden hand that held the glass globe of his old Bristol chair. Under the portraits of the three sages was a shelf. On it, among vacant shells he had found on the beach, lay Pult's *Ta'anit,* Fleg's *Beast.*

He willed them to drift back: not only Mrs. Dorothea Luchs, but also Mrs. Lillian Lebow, Mrs. Edith Horwich, Mrs. Phyllis Kramer, Mrs. Lenore Billiger, Mrs. Vanessa Lichtenberg. Sirens moaning afar, perilous. Mrs. Edith Horwich was short, very young, with infant's cheeks and a cigarette steaming on her lip; Mrs. Phyllis Kramer carried a businesslike note pad, but her shoes were satin, disclosing—despite rain—crimson crescents of toenail; Mrs. Vanessa Lichtenberg's bursting breasts and calves seemed charged with power—yet in her broad face the eyes were as tiny and crumpled as raisins; Mrs. Lenore Billiger, crafty and confidential, had driven in especially, stealing time from her job as a public-health nurse, white as lightning in her uniform; Mrs. Lillian Lebow had stuck in her canvas bag a copy of *Voyager, Glow,* the best-seller about a girl from a poor Lower East Side family who grows up to be a famous Hollywood star.

Mrs. Vanessa Lichtenberg, leaning away, curled her fat shoulders into a hunch—it was as though she was in the grip of a chill.

Common clay, the ordinary article: he did not blame their flesh. But Mrs. Dorothea Luchs had animal beauty.

"Not in the middle of the term," Mrs. Lenore Billiger said. "It doesn't make sense."

"It doesn't make sense," Mrs. Phyllis Kramer said.

"Not in the middle," Mrs. Vanessa Lichtenberg said.

"The term is only a few weeks gone. And it made good sense last year," Brill blew out, pushing them out to sea, "to dismiss Mrs. Fischeltier three weeks before the end of the term. What transpired then, you may recall, was that I was asked to be sensitive to the protests of some of the very same ladies present in this group."

He knew "transpired" was vulgar; that was why he had used it.

"Fischeltier was an idiot," Mrs. Dorothea Luchs said. "She insulted Corinna. She wouldn't let her ask questions. She called Corinna a monopolizer. She said Corinna was running the show. I don't want my kid talked to that way."

This animal beauty of hers was repugnant to Brill; she was as straight as a cat or a boy. Her little mouth was lovely, her flawless teeth more so. Her eyes were as widely spaced as a fawn's—as Claude's. How aggressive she was, how he despised her aggressive energies!

"Fischeltier was an idiot," Mrs. Lenore Billiger said.

"Oh, that idiot Fischeltier," Mrs. Edith Horwich said.

"That fascist," Mrs. Vanessa Lichtenberg said. "And you can't just throw out poor Dina Fifferling after so many years."

Only Mrs. Lillian Lebow, with *Voyager, Glow* sticking out of her canvas bag, had nothing to say. Brill had heard she sometimes called him Frog. Her son, though, was quick. All their children were as quick as starlings.

Mrs. Dorothea Luchs raised her turbulent head. "Forget Fifferling. Fifferling's blood under the bridge, who cares what goes on in third grade? Our kids are graduating, *that's* the point. Besides," she addressed him, "on what basis do you think Sheskin's so able? You've never seen him teach. He's never *taught*."

Principal Brill did not blink. "Ladies"—it was his captain's apostrophe, his loftiest mode—"you understand that Mr. Gorchak himself desired an easing of pressure. I was not to have divulged this, but you force me. Rabbi Sheskin is a young man, and we should give him a chance. Let him show his mettle. Let him aspire. *Ad astra*, ladies, *ad astra!*"

The mothers, receding, scratched at the bit of office carpet with their heels, the delegation turned surly, but Brill kept up his high bright mood until they wore themselves out with contention. How far away they were now! A distant cluster. He had driven them off with a puff.

And only now, in his windmaster's triumph, did he allow himself to see into their secret rooms: it was as if each of the mothers floated inside a darkened doll's house bobbing in the dark dangerous middle of the Phlegethon, and anyone could come and lift the roof on its silvery hinges and look inside—and inside each house there was a bitterness, a hope never to be resolved, crippled ambition, bad books, querulous old parents outliving the cruelty of their prime, the best tableware, an Oriental rug or two, an antique tobacco box, a tragedy, a tragedy!

Still, their children were not disappointing. Their children were as quick as starlings. Even when their children were the ordinary article, they were as quick as starlings.

Thereafter he watched Sheskin. Principal Brill moved quietly along the rear of the classroom and listened to the lesson. He understood at once that the yeshiva student had no obvious personality and appeared to believe in sacred texts. He was like a plain blotter through which the old words seeped. He was also no disciplinarian, and Brill began to suspect that as soon as the awe of unfamiliarity brought on by a new teacher ebbed—four days, five—Gorchak's old classroom would be a howling chaos. Meanwhile the voice was sweet, devoted to the page under the young rabbi's flat fingertips. The eighth grade bent over notebooks, and Brill, stretching out his short neck (heroic, he thought of the sacrifice of Fifferling, the debasement of Gorchak), observed the flowering of a multitude of doodles—tigers, mermaids, planes, supermen, disembodied eyes and teeth, decorative friezes composed of wings and florets. Sheskin reprimanded no one. The doodles went on and on: circles, balloons, eggs, dogs' ears, women's lips and breasts; a kind of trance had set in. The room was in concentration. Old King David was dying. He was dying in this very room. Peering toward Beulah's desk, Brill glimpsed a drawing of a house, with smoke. Immature. He supposed the smoke was rising out of the chimney. The third-graders did that. He looked again: the whole house was on fire, and the trees all around it, even the sky behind—a conflagration.

The third grade, disciplined under Fifferling, under Gorchak remained disciplined. But there was a difference: laughter rolled out the door. "Lowell never fails us," Gorchak shouted out in his bold bland way—he was enjoying himself, he had forgotten the ignominy of moving down. "We can always trust him, he's as good as the clock on the wall. Only instead of tick-tock it's tock-tick. Lowell *always* gets the wrong answer," and out the door the laughter rolled.

A letter came from Dina Fifferling. She bore no grudge against Principal Brill: *he* had always defended her against the assaults of the mothers. But this time—she understood everything exactly—he had broken down under the mothers' pressure. The mothers wanted her out; she was writing to tell him she saw through it all. It was the mothers of the weak pupils. And what, after all, was her sin? She had treated the third grade like little soldiers. She had organized them, straightened their rows, insisted that they keep their notebooks tidy. Clean sheets, headings like even palings. She had made them learn their lists. For the rest of their lives they would remember their vocabulary lists, and *her* conscience, at least, was clear.

Fifferling's letter cheered Brill; it pleased him that she blamed herself. Still, it was stupid to have gotten rid of one of the most reliable of the women teachers. A reckless whim. It was stupid to have hired Sheskin—Brill continued to visit the eighth-grade classroom, and, though the ineluctable hour of brawl and clamor had not yet arrived, there was something dangerously meditative in the air: suspenseful and suspended. It was as if a pillar of the gathered-up lungs of children upheld the ceiling. The young yeshiva student, sweet-voiced, was turning Scripture into story. He was leaving out place names and grammar, everything that Gorchak put in. He breathed at the class with a kind of holy ardor that was unsettling: there was something abnormal, unhealthy, in such piety. He was not rigorous. He was not teaching anything concrete. He was in fact not teaching at all. It was all dreaming and drawing. The mothers would find him out, the commotion would begin.

Brill beckoned the tall new clerk-receptionist into his office and explained how she was to record payments to the new teacher.

Her blue-black ink-moist bangs glowed. "Rabbi Sheskin? He has the quietest class, I've noticed that."

"Have you?" He was annoyed; it was not her place to notice anything beyond her ledgers. She did not seem meticulous; she was somehow florid and flaming. Besides, she had left the door open behind her.

"I think he hypnotizes them in there!" she laughed. "He drugs them! He feeds them grass!"

Her name was the name of a flower. Sometimes he remembered it was Iris; sometimes he thought it was Daisy. He watched her at work in the outer office. She wore glasses with crimson frames, spirals of chains around her neck, and two rings on each hand. She was not serious; her eyes sparked. She had put her son into the first grade.

Brill telephoned Hester Lilt: "I've done something impulsive. I did it two weeks ago. I suppose by now you've heard about it."

"No."

He was certain from the scrape in her throat, the strings of her voice rusted, that he had broken some skein of reflection. But this time he did not apologize.

"Didn't Beulah tell you?"

"Tell me what?"

"The eighth grade has a nice young fellow now. He lets them draw in class. He lets them do anything."

She seemed to gather herself up; she focused. "But wasn't it Mr. Gorchak? What happened to Mr. Gorchak?"

So she knew nothing.

"I got him out of the way. I put him somewhere else.—Didn't Beulah report all this?"

"You got rid of Gorchak?"

"Got him out of the way, yes."

"For Beulah's sake?"

"For yours." He heard the long slow pull of her breath. "Don't worry, I don't think the brainiest can learn anything from the new fellow," he said; this was for a joke.

She said deliberately, "A mistake."

"Doubtless. By next week they'll be running all over him. He's too mild, they'll destroy him."

"The mistake is about Beulah."

"I thought a less acerbic teacher, someone more sympathetic—"

"You write her off."

"She isn't you. Try and see this finally. Give up anguish. I know you suffer," he said.

"Suffer," she repeated. For a moment he thought it was one of her parodies. But she was pointed, severe. "You don't know her. I don't suffer. There's no anguish." He sensed the gathering of a space: she was preparing to stammer. "She's going to be— to be—" He waited without suspense. It was the future she was clawing at; the future was striking her dumb. Then she brought it out: "She's going to be original."

For the first time he pitied her. He said barrenly, "Mrs. Lilt."

"It doesn't matter whether you do anything for her or you don't. It doesn't matter what I do or don't. Nothing like that matters."

"School matters" was all he could say.

"What you are is a schoolmaster," she accused. "What you are is a pedagogue. Your school is a house of worms. Your teachers are eels. Worms and eels. Never mind," she said, "bring Gorchak back if you like, you don't have to do anything for Beulah."

"Only what's suitable. You've seen for yourself how the bright ones are."

"Worms," she answered him, "eels."

Ungrateful: he felt how it was possible to turn against her. Ungrateful, illusioned! She *was* like the others: nature's trick, it comes in with the milk of the teat. Each thinks her own babe is goddess or god. But she was worse than the worst. The worst of them fought. They battled texts, tasks, tests, teachers, schedules, Principal Brill himself: the greed of the teat led them to hope of repair. Hester Lilt was aloof from repair. She believed in a seamless future for her little crippled creature. The others stopped at the present; scratched at the present; intended to force, to refashion, the imperfect present. They had the exuberant reformist ferocity of Cinderella's sisters—they would command the slipper to fit. They would berate it, rail at it, harry it; they would jam their feet into it. Hester Lilt scorned such amelioratives. She was ready to do without the slipper. She was infected with madness. Beulah had made her mad. The flawed daughter, shining, crowned, barefoot, inside the veil of the mother's madness.

T he next week he received from Hester Lilt—in a wide brown envelope carried to school by Beulah, marked BY HAND, and mutely delivered to the clerk-receptionist with the blue-black bangs—a new essay. He surmised that it was a kind of spite. She meant to flatter him. Her flattery was spite, willing at last to acknowledge his homage—how drawn he was to the prodigy of her mind. He was somehow now not so drawn. She intended her genius to punish him.

He pulled the printed sheets out of the envelope and surveyed the title: *On Structure in Silence*. He read:

Silence is not random but shaping. It is like the empty air around the wing, that delineates the wing. . . .

Something came to him then, a clairvoyance, as if he had gotten hold of a thread leading to a great dew-flecked web: fragments of light in a shadowed cranny. If he tugged on a single vein of it, the web would rupture, the drops of light fall into one bright globule. A pool of knowing. He did not go on with it. He crowded the sheets back into their packet; he could not keep his eyes from the new clerk-receptionist's blue-black bangs. Iris or Daisy. He had hired Rabbi Sheskin and the new clerk-receptionist a day apart—she told him this was significant, it made her a sort of twin to Rabbi Sheskin, even though she didn't relate to anything spiritual. Cain wasn't Abel, and that was the whole of her metaphysical learning. She was cheeky with him; he was amazed. It passed through his conscience that the right thing to do would be to sack her; but that was only a whim. Whim after senseless whim. Losing Fifferling, demoting Gorchak, replacing Gorchak, all these loosenings and braidings of his forces laid down as an offering before Hester Lilt—who spurned them. All the same he could do what he pleased, he was a man in possession of an entire society, he was a potentate.

"Daisy," he called into the outer office. "Come here. Shut the door behind you."

She shut the door and stood near him.

"Iris," she said. Petulant. He did not like her to correct him. As if her name made a difference!

"Always shut the door behind you. It's too noisy out there."

"With kids you expect that." The faintest hint of reprimand, like a watercolor smudge. Cheeky!

"Rabbi Sheskin's entries, you've taken care of them?"

"He's all sewed up. He's shipshape."

"I would expect that. And you, are you getting on all right? Do you have any questions?"

She dropped a small round laugh like a button. "Plenty of answers. If you want I could think up questions to go with them."

It did not escape him that she had not once said Principal Brill.

"And your little boy? Is he getting on? You know he's lucky to be in Mrs. Jaffe's class. She's our finest first-grade teacher."

"If she's that good she doesn't get paid all that much."

Cheek! Nerve! He said, "It isn't up to you to question policy here."

"You just now *wanted* questions."

"Not that kind. If you intend to keep the peace"—it was a marvel that he didn't sack her; it was a marvel that his tone was not a club; he heard the cautious diplomacy in it—"you had just better mellow a bit."

"Mellow!" she pounced. "That's an old-people's thing. For your age, not mine."

He knew what was happening—what had already happened. Beneath her ink-moist forehead there were no features that did not seem specially polished. Even the neat round bulb of her nose-tip owned its tiny sheen. Her eyes were ordinary brown, but with the slow incandescence of some old burnished lamp. The walnut-brown hairs of her eyebrows were individually lustrous. Her teeth were bright but crooked, and this crookedness struck his still-foreign vigilance as a curiosity. Three-quarters of his student body were wired, braced, retained; silver links and locks, glittering tracks, plates and flutes weighted and cluttered the teeth of these American children, yet in the new bookkeeper he took in almost victoriously the apparition of a single wayward incisor more forward than the others, with a gleam equal to its prominence. The ceiling light over his desk tapped this stuck-out front tooth and gave him back indecipherable impish semaphores. He understood that she could pounce and bounce, that she was impudent, impertinent—snippy and snappy—insubordinate and cheeky. At the back of her head, when she turned from him, he saw the lambent tarry bun, the little neck, all candid and erect.

"Your little boy," he began.

"Albert."

"Albert," he repeated. He was stunned. A tiny tremor—a tic, really—started in the left half of his upper lip. He struggled to control it but it went on like a vibrato in some alien instrument. He knew what had happened. "Quite so," he said. "Mellowing is for old men like myself. You *do* have all the answers."

The button of laughter fell again. "Not all. Just lots."

"Just lots then. And Albert, does *he* have all the answers?"

Her look grew strict. "Can you tell from first grade what they'll be like all through?"

A flash of Beulah. "Usually," he said.

"Then it's too bad for Albert. It's all up with Albert!" And giggled. A tall woman's laughter is different from that of other women. "But as a matter of fact, if you're speaking of mellow," she told him, "I don't mind older men. My ex-husband was over fifty when we married. After a while I embarrassed him."

Himself embarrassed, Brill could not resist: "Why was that?"

"People thought he was my father."

This devoured him. That glinting forward tooth with its childish spell. He was riven to the naked bone. He knew what had happened. What had happened had no name. He would not be promiscuous with the name it did not have. It was a seizure more terrible than any other. The little neck, all candid and erect.

"Did you mind," he asked, "when they took him for your father?"

"*He* minded."

He was relieved. "Shut the door after you," he said; he would not have minded.

He went to his safe and took out Dr. Glypost's report:

ALBERT CHARLES GARSON,
AGE SIX YEARS THREE MONTHS

A likable small dark boy with bright eyes and much open charm, he did not hesitate during the Rorschach test. His responses were standard but usually leaning toward the healthily optimistic. He is alert, humorous, quick and spunky at everything, if not necessarily accurate. He is right-handed, more oral than verbal. His intelli-

cheekiness. He liked it when she was aroused and talked back. He thought how his sisters would recognize such spirit as akin to their own—no matter that they were across the sea, growing elderly in an ancient city. Iris Garson was pert and bold and young; but she was also brave. She was brave enough to ask him to her little flat, an attic in a converted house rather a long way off from school. A large noisy Greek family owned the house and lived below, on the first and second floors and in the basement. She sat him down in the kitchen and cooked him a simple fish dinner, prettily served on flowered china. It was a Sunday afternoon, and the good-natured bellowing of the Greeks underneath made the table rattle. Her little boy was not at home; he had gone to play ball with a classmate. "You know," Brill told her, "you'll have to get Albert out of here before long." "Why is that?" she asked, stopping with her fish on her fork. "When he gets a little older. The racket you have here. These rowdies. He won't do well if he hasn't got a quiet place to study." "The Papageorgious have six children," she said, "and the oldest daughter has two of her own, and they all live together. What a bachelor you are! More a bachelor than a principal. Kids have to be noisy. It's life. You don't know anything about children," she said; no one, not even Mrs. Dorothea Luchs, had ever dared to say anything like this to him, though he had often seen it in the mothers' faces. "I think I'm smarter than you are, no matter how much you know about education, even if I can't say stars in Latin." "Oh," he said, "you *are* just that." "Just what?" "Something luminous. Shining," he explained. "Then I'd better go powder my nose." "Your nose always *does* shine. I like it." "My ex-husband didn't. He said my complexion was like a teenager's." He stood at the side of the sink as she washed the dishes, carefully receiving each one to dry in a towel covered with blue violets. The kitchen nearly swayed, vibrating, enveloped in a grand barbaric pounding: one of the Papageorgiou boys was playing some artificial-sounding instrument with Brobdingnagian electronic amplification. In the middle of these tumultuous blasts

Brill, holding a little blue cup, was more serene than at any time since the days when he dipped his head down into the great tractates of Gemara; he had been happy when Rabbi Pult praised him. From the hour that Claude named him Dreyfus he had never been happy at the University. He had never been happy with telescopes or in the years of obscure teaching in Milwaukee. (And in between, the cellar, the hayloft.) His sisters always said he had no capacity for happiness because he had no capacity for decision. Yet when he decided to leave the observatory in Paris for the middle of America, how they grumbled! He held the little blue cup while the waves of clamor beat, withdrew, and again riotously beat; he felt perfectly happy. "You want to get Albert out of here," he said again; "he won't be able to study." "Albert isn't much of a studier. What he likes is baseball. That's why he's over at Stevie's, for practice." She reflected; it made her eyes dim. He was not used to seeing them without their spark. She asked, "Where would we go?" "Come to me," he said.

So they worked it out between them. She called him Joseph for the first time; she had never once said Principal Brill. When he was leaving she sang down the stairs after him, "You're so self-important! You think you're absolutely somebody!"—because he had spoken that way about Albert. And then, right through the Papageorgious' racket, "You won't mind that Albert isn't a studier?" He gave no answer. She would not have heard him anyhow.

Several mornings afterward he stopped Mrs. Jaffe at her classroom door. "How is Albert Garson getting on?"

Mrs. Jaffe was an honest woman. She was on the Scriptural side of the Curriculum, like Gorchak; but she said nothing about work. "The children like him. He makes friends. I suppose he could have more imagination."

Normal. It is normal not to have too much imagination. At the same time he wished Mrs. Jaffe cared more about real work, like Gorchak. There were too many posters in her room. He put his head in to find Albert. It was difficult to pick him out—the small boys, in their plaid shirts and sober-colored pants, all looked alike. The girls seemed more particularized. When he recognized Iris's son he was pleased by how pretty he was: a sweet firm little neck like his mother's, and a rapid smile. It bothered him that the smile was so rapid, so recurring, so perpetual. Sometimes it is necessary not to smile. As usual Mrs. Jaffe's hands were white with papier-mâché. She had acquired her miniature celebrity through her elbows and her feet, which she turned this way and that in order to demonstrate the shapes of the letters of the Hebrew alphabet. He thought of Fifferling's solid sheets of vocabulary lists: as solid and concrete as bricks. What a loss, what a fool he was, to have driven out Fifferling, like Hagar, for the sake of Hester Lilt's child!

He telephoned Hester Lilt. The familiar croak, the barb, the dark bird's caw of dark Europe—it settled into his ear strangely now; his ear was full of lightness and cheek. Iris giggled often; she was a scandal among the secretaries. He had made her promise to say nothing; she was not to call him Joseph where anyone could hear. He too would soon be a scandal. The scandal was only waiting for the mothers to sniff it out. It seemed to him one or two already suspected, and were signaling romantic eyes at each other in parody.

He had planned how this conversation would go. It would be purposeful—he had his news to get to. He said, "Mrs. Lilt." He gave her his courtliest tone: "It was so good of you to let Beulah bring me your paper"—and then disliked himself for it. Preening, self-important!

There was no response, or else an invisible bewilderment; at length a strange little burst. "Yes! That paper! I forgot I sent you that, it was ages ago, Beulah took it—" She stopped. "Was it hard going?"

"You don't think well of my capacities," he said in the same embroidered, heavy, preening way, "if you ask me that." Oh, self-important, he thought he was absolutely somebody! "The truth is"—already he felt out of control, he felt she was pressing him to confess something against his will—"I haven't gotten into the meat of it."

"You mean you haven't read it."

"*Nihil est veritatis luce dulcius*," he said. "Not yet."

"You won't and you can't."

There was a bruise in her voice he had not heard before. She was bruised and bruising. He detected some new belligerence. The day of the birthday she had lost herself, she was all fragments. She was different now. She was hard. He had not expected this; it made an obstacle. He wanted to come to his news. "I *will* read you," he said, conciliatory. "I always read you."

"And then you praise. *Absolvo te*. When you read me, no matter what it is, you compliment me afterward. I don't want to be complimented."

She was pushing him out of the way of his intention. "I haven't called to give compliments," he protested.

"Then it's to give insults. You want to talk about Beulah."

How brutal she was! How brutal she made him appear! "No," he said, "not Beulah." But this too seemed wrong; he tried to undo it. "Is she happier now? Beulah? Rabbi Sheskin always praises her drawings."

"Is Mr. Gorchak happier now? Wherever you've put him?"

"It's impossible to talk to you."

"First it's impossible to read me, now it's impossible to talk to me! What's to be done, am I so inaccessible—"

"You're being hard on me," he said.

"Yes."

"You sent that paper with Beulah just for that, just to be hard."
"Oh yes," she said.

It was as if she was calculating, weighing. All he wanted was to give his news! He asked, with so much simplicity that now no one could call him self-important, "Why are you being hard on me?"

"You don't proceed. You're glued in place. You're a man who stops too soon. You deduce the future from the present. All despots do. You're stuck."

He listened to this caravan with all his attention. "I have it in mind," he said, "to be married." He waited. He heard nothing. "You can't say I'm stuck. It's May and December, that's not being stuck." Again he waited. "After all these years," he said finally, earnestly, "I'm to become ordinary."

"You were never extraordinary."

She had cut him but he did not bleed. "Not in your way, no." He meant he was abnormal in his own way, in the way of a man who has had a hidden life. He did not mind it that she had called him a despot. "You think I'm a fool to want a wife. At my age."

"Is it a wife you want?"

"What else would I want?"

"A child."

"Oh yes," he said, "yes. She's young enough for that. May and December, I told you. She already has a son. She was married before, I don't mind that. A first-grader, a nice pretty little boy."

"Is *she* very pretty?"

"Oh yes, very pretty. A nice simple little woman. She's not afraid of anything."

"You mean she doesn't flatter you."

He laughed freely now. "She's intrepid!" He wondered all at once whether Hester Lilt was jealous. He asked himself whether he had telephoned her just for that—to learn whether she would be jealous. A lone woman with a child. Her position was exactly the same as the new clerk-receptionist's. The receiver was moist with the sweat of his hold on it. He wished he had gone to see her instead. If he had gone to see her the tumble of her whitening hair would have reassured him: she was more than twenty years older than Iris. "She has a nice quick little brain," he went on, "the ordinary article. Not a deep thinker—she'll do very well for me. The boy's name is Albert. Albert Charles Garson. I suppose I could adopt him. In fact it has the sound of a Hohenzollern princeling, don't you think? Albert Charles Garson Brill?"

"The simple little woman has a simple little child," Hester Lilt said.

"He isn't my child, he won't ever be my child," he let out. "But if *we* have a child—" He was embarrassed; he was used to the official "we," not this naked one; he was confused; this "we," sent through the wires straight to Hester Lilt, shocked.

"If the simple little woman with the simple little child bears another simple little child. And it's yours." She was deepening her blade. "*That's* what eats you. You worry about being father to the ordinary article."

He said nothing.

"You wouldn't be able to take it, is that it? I know how attracted you are to the heights. *Ad astra*. The heights or nothing."

"I've had enough of nothing," he said. "I've had years of nothing. A whole tract. A lifetime."

"Then there's nothing left to say," she said with her terrible clarity.

Now he could begin to bleed. He stumbled after her: "You can take it."

"Take what?"

"Beulah." His throat failed him. He brought out a voiceless call. "Tell me how you take it."

"Don't come to me with that! I knew from the start it would lead to Beulah! It's Beulah you're after! You want to hear how I bear up, you think she's an affliction!"

"It's an affliction," he said, "not to be like you."

"Oh, sweet! With that kind of sentiment you ought to propose to *me*."

He heard her hesitate just long enough to let his breath flow into the gap. "Sometimes," he admitted, "I've almost thought of it. But I stopped." He could not tell whether he was prevaricating—was it true? Had he ever almost thought of this? "What you are made me stop. You're too elevated. You're too clever. You're too acute."

"I'm too old."

He said slowly into the instrument, "I want my own son. I want someone to say kaddish for me when I die. —I want to be normal."

"Then get married."

He knew it was a barb. "I want that," he said, all the same.

"It's not a wife you want. It's not a child you want. It's yourself," she contradicted. "Yourself continued. Yourself redeemed. You put yourself at the center. You've been looking into the grave. You want immortality."

Now it was quiet between them. She could not see that he was sick of immortality. He had had his fill of perpetuity. She was obtuse about immortality, she was obtuse about her child. He let a minute pass. He resumed his proper throat. He said with his full voice—not forceful or loud, still very quiet, but whole, "You've never accepted it about Beulah. You've never understood about Beulah and yourself. If you'd ever understood about Beulah and yourself you would know what it is I'm afraid of. Because I'm afraid, I'm a coward—"

"You *are* a coward," she flung out. "You want to know everything in advance—every twist, every contingency, isn't that right? You want to know how things turn out. You want to know how to manage fate, only because once upon a time fate managed you. You think because they saved you in the convent, you've earned salvation forever. After that, no more sullying! The end of stain. No more sorrow. You want to know how to manage"—she spread out a length of her own laughter with so much wide distrust that he was able to perceive how it differed in every grain from Iris's busy gurgle—"anguish. Anguish, that's your word for it! Never mind anguish over the graveyards of the world! Anguish over school failure is what you don't want! What you can't swallow! It won't go down your gullet! Principal Brill can't be put in a position where he might have to flunk the fruit of his own loins! Tell me—am I right? Am I right? Say it!" She was panting; he heard it clearly. *"You've* never understood about Beulah! Never! What you've done is write her off, I told you! Only a coward would write her off! You and your cockatoo teachers, your lackeys, your eels and worms! Gorchaks and Seelenhohls, the ignorant, the ignorant!"

He hated it that they had the telephone between them now. He thought what it would be like to see her face in passion—her scholarly face, with its small eyes and tiny glimmering wart, its heavy innocent chin; he wanted to fight her.

He said, "You think I'm a fool but I'll show you how clever I am. I have my limitations but I can be clever."

"You must be clever. You read me."

"Read you! Exactly! That's the point, I read you! That last thing Beulah brought, what's it called—Structure—Silence—"

"But that's just the one you didn't read," she said neatly.

"Dead! Silent! That's how she came! A deaf-mute! Always like that! You see what I'm telling you? Your daughter carrying this—this Silence, and like a deaf-mute hands it to Iris, never opens her mouth—so I found you out. Just then. Then and there. I found you out. I'm onto the secret of your brain—"

"Iris?" she broke in. "Is she the one?"

"My fiancée. Office clerk, plain and simple. My bride," offering her these words like a sacrifice: she would despoil them, she would scorn them.

"Principal Brill's bride," she murmured with this new scoffing passion of hers. "The secret of *my* brain? Why not tell the secret of the bride's? Or is there no secret because there is no—"

"Mrs. Lilt!" he yelled. "The fact is I've got you deciphered! Decoded! I know where it comes from! Imagistic linguistic logician, the whole mouthful of it!" He was making himself stolid against her. He was making himself brave. "Everything you say or invent or think or write," he pressed, "comes out of Beulah. You're listening to the truth. It all comes out of Beulah."

She cried, "Leave out Beulah!"

"All your metaphysics. All your philosophy. All your convictions. All out of Beulah. You justify her," he said. "You invent around her. You make things fit what she is. You surround her. I'm onto you! If Beulah doesn't open her mouth, then you analyze silence, silence becomes the door to your beautiful solution, that's how it works! If Beulah can't multiply, then you dream up the metaphor of a world without numbers. My God—metaphor! Image! Theory! You haven't *got* any metaphors or images or theories. All you've got is Beulah. Any idea of yours—look into it, look right *at* it, and what you'll see is the obverse of Beulah. Wherever there's a hole in her—a deficiency, a depression, a dent, an absence—you produce a bump. You make up something to suit the hole, to account for it. You compensate for everything. You re-tailor the universe. You haven't got any ideas. You've only got Beulah."

How hollow his voice was in the instrument! But he kept it up. "Now," he said—what a triumph—"*now* am I stopping too soon? Now haven't I gone all the way?" It was as if, inside the tunnel of their little black baal, she was meditating and meditating. What a satisfaction, what bliss, it would be to gaze at her now, to gaze for a long time!

"Don't tell me I still haven't gone far enough!" he said. "The last consequence isn't too far—isn't this Hester Lilt's own principle? Carry every image to its ultimate turn? Leave out nothing? Don't succumb to earliness! Never stop too soon! And that's the reason you've been able to bear it—the disappointment. Because you've made use of it. Without Beulah to show the way you wouldn't have a subject matter! A thesis! Without Beulah where would you get your ideas about pedagogy? About silence? About emptiness? You'd be a barren pot! You'd be no more glorious than some little teacher trying to put over a scrap of geography without a map! You *need* her! You need her to be nothing, so you can be something. She's Genesis Chapter One, Verse Two—*tohu vavohu*, unformed and void, darkness over the deep, so you can spin out your Creation from her!—Remember that joke of yours, how you called yourself *chaos ex machina?* It wasn't a joke. You call *me* despot! Look how you use, you eat, you cannibalize your own child!"

He understood then that she had hung up some time ago. The air in the receiver weighed empty in his hand. Void. And after that Principal Brill's life went quickly, quickly. He was astonished at how quickly it could go now. Everything became a plan. He put away his sneakers. He had no time to run in the mornings; he had no time at all. The new clerk-receptionist looked over his dark rooms; she did not like them, and this pleased him and gave him hope. "It's true, they're not habitable," he said; "we'll get ourselves a decent place," and he began to enumerate the neighboring suburbs and their advantages and drawbacks, speculating on which would be the most suitable. "I thought you said you have to stay here on account of the contract," Iris said. "I'll get them to change it. After all," he said, "those terms were set long ago, and we've got different circumstances now." "Oh," she reflected, "I don't know. I can see the possibilities. We could do a lot if we took out all these little windows. A conversation piece, what d'you think?—the idea of living in a hayloft." He had never told her about the other hayloft; she knew he had been hidden in the war, but she was young, and all that seemed as distant to her as Attila the Hun. She was uninterested in his recountings of old desolations. The nuns especially (he had undertaken to tell about the convent) bored her. "Books!" she said. "The whole world was being bombed and all that, and there you were with mounds and mounds of books! Reading!" This shamed him; it was the truth, he had never suffered at all. Fleg underground, how was that a vexation? He had endured a miracle, an idyll. Even the time in the farmer's hayloft was lucky; luckier for him than for most. He saw how she was right: their lives were for the plucking now, why go digging up ancient suppurations? She loathed it when he lapsed into French: but there were so many ways to adore her in his own tongue, how could he resist? "It's creepy, I wish you'd quit," she scolded; "whenever you talk up your nose like that, it feels as if you're talking to somebody else; somebody you knew long ago; somebody in history. *I'm* not in history!" she cried. And she was not. She accompanied him to the Board meeting and spoke up all on her own, with so much bravery and charm that it was less than five minutes to full victory: she wheedled them into more lumber than had gone into the first renovation, when the elderly benefactress had skimped (she argued) on this and that; and besides, by now everything needed modernization. And then she worked on the renovation plans with such gusto that he had to laugh out loud: these energies of hers! The little windows were removed, and new huge ones framed out, for the light. Walls had to be broken through—all at once his warren, his carrels, were transformed into spacious galleries. He marveled at two big bathrooms and a resplendent kitchen. The ceilings and floors were showing an elasticity he had never suspected. He slept among carpenters' debris, broken sticks, powdery old plaster, but in reality he did not sleep much; there was so little time, there was so much to buy. A new table, a bureau, many new chairs, a new bed.

And still they called it the hayloft.

Iris worried about Albert. He was not doing well in the first grade. He was too easy-going, he wanted to have fun. She wondered if they should put him in a different school, a simpler one, not so pressured and competitive, without a Dual Curriculum—but how could they, how would it look for Principal Brill's soon-to-be-stepson to have to go away? Brill offered to adopt Albert. She was uncertain. She felt he did not like to give his name to a little boy who wasn't smart enough even for the baby stuff in the first grade. They tumbled the question between them, but they were very busy, there was no time to think properly, there was so much to be done. They decided to announce their engagement in May, around Commencement time; but the commotion in the hayloft had already announced everything, the news was already out, the mothers were already chattering and making eyes, the doctors were already mocking with coarse fingers and shaming jokes, already the wedding presents were beginning to come in.

In April Brill told Iris that he had consulted with Dr. Glypost. Albert was almost seven. He was too old to change identities—it would affect his whole future outlook. It would harm his libido. He should keep his own name, and not become Albert Charles Garson Brill, a Hohenzollern princeling. "A who and *what?*" Iris said; she did not understand. "Dr. Glypost thinks he should be left alone, he shouldn't be adopted." "Oh," Iris said. The sheen ebbed from her eyes. "Why did you say that German-sounding thing? Isn't that the name of a composer? I used to play the 'Surprise Symphony' on the piano—it's by a German composer, do you think Albert might have an aptitude for music?" She watched Albert all the time now; she watched his aptitudes. She stood over him while he did his homework and she would not let him go out to throw his ball. She shouted at the Papageorgious, and told them not to shout—Albert had to study. The boy with the amplified electric guitar said something ugly, and after that she would not speak to any of the Papageorgious. She instructed Albert to keep away from all of them, no matter how much he liked to play with the oldest daughter's second baby. She wished Brill would make the carpenters hurry up, so she and Albert could get away from the Papageorgious; you couldn't hear yourself think in such a house. Albert was upset; Mrs. Jaffe scolded him because he kept forgetting yesterday's lesson; he was eating too much cake, and getting fat.

Over three decades it had rained only four times on Commencement day. This year the eighth grade's perennial luck held. It was a beautiful evening—the lawns newly mowed, brightly verdant, the crickets yelping high. The Phlegethon simmered black and red. In a certain deep stone-littered dell where the mower could not go without endangering its axle, the uncut dandelions in their hundreds burned yellow as butter. The little incline above the Phlegethon made a natural dais; Principal Brill sat up there on a folding chair, flanked by Gorchak and Seelenhohl, while young Rabbi Sheskin tapped the microphone on the lectern; he blew into it with such a noise that the guests, spread over the fields, turned. Then Seelenhohl went down the hill toward the lip of the lake, to organize the march: first the Color Guard, recruited from the seventh grade, then the eighth-grade girls two by two, followed by the eighth-grade boys, also two by two. The choir—the whole fifth grade—was testing its uneasy throat under the darkling eaves of the chair factory. Brill heard them tuning up: *Eliyahu ha-navi, Eliyahu ha-tishbi, Eliyahu, Eliyahu, Eliyahu ha-giladi*; and then *The Minstrel bo-o-oy to the wars is gone*; and then *Chevaliers de la Table Ronde, goûtons voir si le vin est bon, goûtons voir, oui oui oui!* Elijah the Tishbite, the Knights of the Round Table, the bards of the Old World . . . ah, how he fell with these into the poetry side of life, into the swarm of small pure voices. The dusk was coming down now, and the fathers had begun to flash their cameras like fireflies. The guests settled on rows and rows of folding chairs—behind them the field, already growing dusk-gray, over which the graduates would trail; and, beyond, the blackening beach, the water slashed red by the sun's last track. Somewhere among the mothers Iris sat under her blue-black ink-moist bangs, shining; she rejoiced in the scandal of being Principal Brill's first and only bride, the bride of his old age. They had totted up all the others—the Misses Feibush, Springer, Whitehill, Trittschuh, Tepperbaum, all those others whom no one of a decent vintage could recollect by now, faces and names and occupations and gifts lost along with the zealous matchmakers of early generations; and the phantom sweetheart destroyed in the blitz (or in the Resistance, or in Poland), on whose account Brill had, romantically, never married. Mimi Feibush, they recalled, had played the piano, and was particularly remembered for being a social worker with intellectual tendencies; Sylvia Tepperbaum used to do watercolors, and very nicely; Elaine Springer was known in her prime for having a perfect complexion, and still he had passed her by. These were all fine ample women now, the mothers of lawyers and professors, and Elaine Springer, in fact, was the grandmother of fraternal twins, one girl and one boy: Lori and Larry. And still he had passed them all by: until *this* one, with a saucy tooth and no prettier than any of the others, a divorcée! Her little boy was running wild; Mrs. Bloomfield had to reach out and squash him down into a seat, because the March from *Aïda* had started—the first star was out—and the eighth-grade girls were rising (so it appeared) out of the enchanted lake-waters, sailing slowly up the middle aisle, two by two, over the shuddering grass in their alabaster gowns, clasping their nosegays, up the slope toward Principal Brill. He saw the doctors kneeling handsomely, like the young knights of the Table, with their beepers on their belts, pointing complicated-looking cameras, which now and then violently flashed. He saw Mrs. Dorothea Luchs, Mrs. Vanessa Lichtenberg, Mrs. Lillian Lebow, Mrs. Phyllis Kramer, Mrs. Edith Horwich, Mrs. Lenore Billiger, Mrs. Maxine Gould, side by side in the same row; and he saw their sons and daughters, Gregory Horwich the tallest boy, Howard Kramer the smallest; he saw Corinna Luchs and her pack, all of them spiraling like seraphim up the hillock toward him, a gossamer squad of innocents and teary beauties. Beulah Lilt went by, her pale hair captured at the temples by a white band—he put out his hand to something invisible, as if his finger might poke straight through. "Is your mother here?" She nodded, with startled eyes, then set one foot tensely in front of the other so as not to fall out of step with *Aïda*. In her flossy little gown he could hardly tell her apart from the other white-banded forms moving solemnly near. Then it was time to deliver his address into the microphone, standing at the lectern; after that he announced the awards for academic excellence. Again and again Corinna Luchs mounted the hill to applause; so did Ronnie Lebow and Becky Gould, but not so often as Corinna; Corinna was the Class Valedictorian. She came to the microphone and read her speech. "We, the newest graduates of our beloved school, look forward with confidence to our happy future," she began, "with gratitude to our honored teachers and parents, and to our esteemed Principal, whose gracious words, *ad astra*, will remain with us for many years"—she had once told Mrs. Seelenhohl her ambition was to be a pilot and ride in the air. It was Brill's thirty-fourth Commencement ceremony; they were all alike; he was fatigued. During the course of his address—in his own ears how paltry, how indifferent—he did not remember about Iris; he was thinking of Hester Lilt.

The exercises ended in the dark. There was a scuttling, a trampling, a tumult of voices, cars splattering gravel, handshakes, shrieks, spilled ice cream, streamers; Iris stood beside him, a consort; he was bewitched by how she teased him in front of all the mothers. And really now they did not seem at all like adversaries—they gathered around Iris as if she was some curious little bird from a far continent. Then the little bird summoned up its banter and its prattle, and everyone laughed, with such good will, and looked at him in a way they had never looked at him before. They asked him new kinds of questions—whether the wedding would be large or small, which rabbi would preside, how the reconstruction of the hayloft was coming along, and how many bedrooms it had: suddenly he was being treated like a young man everyone was interested in—like a bridegroom—and he knew it was because of Iris, who bent her head so naturally, so sweetly and winningly, and had such a proud radiance, which she shook out like wings opening. Albert scurried by, and Iris swooped him up and kept him by her, and everyone smiled at him as if he was the most important little person they had ever seen. Then the new graduates ran up, carrying their autograph books, and Principal Brill had to sign each one, and Iris had to sign too, just as if she was one of the teachers; she wrote the same thing in every book— "Good Luck for Your Future 'Hi-School' Years"—and he was not annoyed by this or even by her handwriting, which was almost like printing, very firm and simple and straight-up-and-down, only with a round porthole instead of a dot over the *i*. He felt at home with her handwriting, even with the porthole. She was what he expected her to be, a kind-hearted and sensible person whom everybody liked. He drove her to the Papageorgious' house—they no longer called it *hers*—and he knew that because of Albert's bedtime (he had to be sung to every night, sometimes for more than an hour) Iris would send him away; if he stayed he would scold her for making Albert infantile.

When he turned back into the school grounds—it was deep night now, the trees were black, and through the lakewind-fragrant air he could hear the remote clack-clack of the truckmen folding the chairs and loading them—he noticed someone hurrying alone down the private road that led to the highway. With accusatory brightness his headlights picked out a large woman walking almost as quickly in her own direction as his engine was moving him in his. In the brilliant beam her uncovered hair stood up stark white: it was Hester Lilt. She had grown wider; her chin seemed broader, her shins stouter. It was eight months since she had put the receiver down without his knowing. He never telephoned her again. Her books lay in a box. The essay Beulah brought him was still in a drawer of his desk, but he had never looked at it since. He never thought of her—only just tonight, in the middle of his address; he did not like supposing Hester Lilt might sit there damning him, when all he meant to say was what any other principal would say. Gratulation and aspiration, repetition and convention, no different from all the years before—only that he had left out *ad astra*. Mrs. Dorothea Luchs expected him to put it in—that was why she had made Corinna put it in; but he had left it out. During the ceremony he forgot he was an engaged man. There was no honor or award of any kind for Hester Lilt's daughter, no mention of any kind, she was invisible; the mother could not be surprised. He judged it better to pass her by on the road; then he was sorry. "Hey!" he called. "What's the matter? Don't you have a ride?" She did not own a car.

"Everyone's gone."

"Isn't Beulah with you?"

"She's over at the Luchses'—a graduation party. Corinna's mother took them all over there in a station wagon. She was going to drop me off at the bus stop, but she forgot—I don't know, maybe there wasn't any room. And all the other parents left before, because the girls were dawdling—"

"You've been stranded."

"It's all right, I'll find the bus."

"How does Beulah get home?"

"They're all staying for the night. A slumber party."

He drove on, concentrating, until he came to the graveled parking field. Then he wheeled slowly round and caught up with her; she was already approaching the highway.

"I'll take you home."

"All right."

He could not decide whether or not it was right to speak. For five minutes he drove and said nothing. She kept her head turned to the open window. He felt he had the manners of a bridegroom, everything he chose to do was becoming, so he said, "Beulah looked sweet."

"Oh yes. They all did."

"Did you get to meet Iris?"

"No. But some of the others were looking at her. I talked to Mrs. Lichtenberg—she said such interesting things."

He had never known Mrs. Lichtenberg to say an interesting thing. "About Iris?"

"About Iris, yes."

Her house was not far; they were quiet again.

He ventured, "Has Beulah decided where she's going to high school?"

"I'm afraid I've decided for her."

"Mrs. Seelenhohl thinks she ought to go to the Academy. They keep up something like our Dual Curriculum and they're not so rough on them there."

"I've enrolled her somewhere else."

He stopped at her door. "In the neighborhood?"

"We're leaving the country," she told him, and got out of the car.

He took this in for a long time. "Where are you going?"

"Well, you'll laugh. I would if I were you. I've been invited to take a post in Paris." She was standing on the sidewalk, speaking through the window.

He thought of his sisters. "A post? There can't be a Department of Imagistic Linguistic Logic—"

Now she laughed herself. "They call it *se faire des idées*. But it comes to the same."

"*Irréprochable.* I suppose you'll get your real recognition over there."

"I've had quite enough over here. I haven't been an American for a dozen years for nothing."

"I've been one for nothing for three dozen. But over there they'll be more in tune. They'll suit you better. Europe," he said, "is Europe." He put his hand on the wheel, to turn it from the curb; instead he switched the motor off and filled his lungs. He said: "You hung up on me."

She pushed her head through the car window and peered at him with her small eyes; he saw the little white wart.

"And now you've begun," she said.

"Begun?"

"Having the child."

"That's in God's hands, isn't it?" he asked. "Whether we have one." He said this outright; now he had no fear of the "we."

"You haven't begun? Mrs. Lichtenberg said she's sure you've begun."

He shut his mouth. He opened his mouth. "Good Lord, nine weeks!"

"She says the mothers can tell."

How he despised these lactating beasts! "It's one of those mishaps. We've kept it to ourselves, God knows. Nothing shows, you saw that—"

"The look on your face shows."

"Old wives' tales, I don't *have* a look."

"Not the kind they think."

"What kind?"

"Terror."

He recognized her little revenge. He said: "Why did you hang up on me?" His lungs were all at once dry and in pain. "I told you, I can't go through what you've been through."

"I haven't been through anything." She said peaceably, "I'm only waiting."

"I couldn't live with a child like that. Not if it was one of my own."

"What *could* you live with?"

"Intelligence, intelligence!" he cried.

She withdrew her head from the car window. "I wish you what you wish yourself," she said; she was already a few yards off. "I'm sure that's the fairest thing."

He sat in his dismantled rooms for more than an hour, looking at the broken walls; then he telephoned Iris. She had been asleep and woke into sourness. He explained that a trouble hung over them, a genuine scandal, not the playful one of the difference in their years. Everyone knew she was with child. "We're getting married in eight days, Joseph, where's the scandal? That's silly." She liked this excitement. She liked it! It came to him that it was she who had told the mothers. "Go to bed, Joseph. I'm exhausted, I just barely got Albert to sleep. I thought you got home ages ago."

"I had to drive one of the parents. She was stranded on the road."

"Which one was that?"

"Mrs. Lilt."

"I don't know that one. I never saw that one. You've done your good deed for the night, Joseph, so go to bed."

The wedding was private and very small. All the secretaries were invited, to please Iris, and Brill asked Gorchak, because Gorchak had been longest in the school. Just before the little ceremony (the bride stood considerably taller than the groom), Brill told Gorchak that next year he could have the eighth grade back. Rabbi Sheskin would take the third. Gorchak said he held no grudge and nothing was lost, because in no more than the space of a single term, and in spite of youth and seeming mildness, Rabbi Sheskin had established, with old-timers like himself (Gorchak often forgot that his own years were not heavy), a respectable reputation for firmness; Sheskin must be a first-rate stickler, since he had kept Gorchak's old room every bit as quiet as Gorchak ever did—he knew how to control them. "I just hope he isn't too harsh. It's *too* quiet in there. He should develop more of a sense of humor and get them to laugh," Gorchak said.

"Ephraim," Iris called, "here we are about to have a baby and get married, and all you can talk about is your own popularity!"

In July they flew to Paris, to show Brill's sisters his bride and her little boy. The ABCs had grown elderly; he saw how they bickered, and how they took ironic aim at one another. Joseph and Iris and Albert stayed in an inexpensive hotel up the street from the block of flats where Anne and Claire lived uneasily together, and every day visited these plump old spinsters for tea. Berthe joined them, tumbling out of buses, embracing fat bundles from the *pâtisserie*. She had bought the most costly cakes, iced in every color, tarts bursting with chocolate and lemon cream. Anne whispered to him behind the door, "She's gone showy on us. It's all out of her dead husband's shoes." Claire had written how Berthe had returned to Paris after Glassman's death; poor Berthe was now a widow. It was true the Hungarian refugee had left her not badly off. But not for a single moment would she consider moving in with her sisters, *non!* The neighborhood was not fashionable enough; the *pâtisserie* was not fancy enough. Besides, according to Berthe, once a woman has had a husband, she can never again live with other women, particularly the unmarried; in the case of Madame Glassman, two husbands in her past, it was twice as unlikely. Berthe had a large flat of her own in a much nicer *quartier.*

Of the three, Berthe, despite her bereavement, seemed the cheeriest. She said what a funny honeymoon it was—a bright young *maman* and a *papa* in his sixties and a small *garçon* and a

new *bébé* on the way (*kayn aynhore*). All the sisters were delighted
with Iris and instantly fond of Albert. They crammed him with
croissants and *gâteaux* and said there was nothing so promising
for future looks as a round-cheeked handsome stout little chap,
with good thick baby-fat suitable for love-pinches. It was clear to
Iris (who considered herself sharp about such things) that there
was bad blood between Berthe and the others, but Albert endured
his love-pinches with so much egalitarianism that it appeared to
unite all three of them; they said his name the French way, Al-
bair, they commanded him to call them Tante Anne, Tante Claire,
Tante Berthe, and arranged excursions with an efficiency that
astonished Brill. For their age they were reasonably energetic and
extremely enthusiastic, and they dragged Albert everywhere to see
the sights. "For once Berthe's fat purse is good for something,"
Anne whispered behind the door, "besides just showing off."

They took Albert to the top of the Eiffel Tower, they took him
to the Bois de Boulogne, they took him for a boat ride under all
the bridges of the Seine. They showed him the Bastille—nothing
but a column—and then descended into the Métro, to emerge on
the Champs-Elysées. They showed him the twin steeples of Notre
Dame and the Arc de Triomphe. They took him to the Opéra,
with its staircase and painted ceiling and palatial illumination,
and to the Rex cinema—he was fonder of the Rex than of *William
Tell*. They gawked at the Elysée Palace, the waxworks in Mont-
martre, the mountain goats in the Parc Zoologique. They even
took him in a hired car (paid for by Berthe) out of town to
Versailles, and when they asked him—standing in the Sun King's
Hall of Mirrors—what he liked best of all his adventures, he said
it was the croissants.

One afternoon Anne caught a summer cold—she thought it
was from the river spray; the day on the Seine had been Claire's
idea—so Claire went with Albert to the Rue Amelot, to see the
equestrian acts; after that, she promised, they would stop at a
pâtisserie, and then they would go again to the Rex. Berthe came

and pulled Iris out to try the shops—Iris grumbled that the stores here were too expensive and couldn't compare; they had better things at home. "Wait! You haven't seen the shoes on the Faubourg St. Honoré!" cried cheery Berthe; she knew a *bottier* Glassman's factory had sold to, where they would treat Madame Glassman with special consideration, in honor of her husband's memory.

Brill stayed behind and had a cup of tea with Anne; then she burrowed about for her hot-water bottle and slid down under the quilt with it. He fell back into the rocking chair beside her bed: it was his first chance to talk alone with one of the sisters. Memory burned in his kidney. The brown brine-bottles, Gabriel and Loup, *maman* and *papa*, Michelle, Leah-Louise, Rabbi Pult, Ruth's little fingernails—it struck him that Ruth would have been a woman in her forties now. He could not swallow the burning. "Hanna," he said, using their old family name for Anne; but he stopped. He looked at the bed. Too pale, too frail, too crushed, too horribly creased, her hag's mouth wide and snorting, his worn sister lay asleep; old, exhausted, far from history.

Left on his own, he climbed on a bus and let it take him where it would. It puzzled him to hear, from the throats of these ordinary passengers, the tremors of his own language. It was both normal and not normal. Intimacies of lost cadences! Out of the throats of a whole population! For the first time he knew where he was. He knew where he wanted to be. He asked the driver for directions, hopped off, boarded another bus, got off at the corner, walked halfway into a deserted street, and stood before the convent gate. He stood a long while, staring at the front door so steadily that his lower lids began to smart, as if from an absence of blinking. No one came in or out. The place seemed no longer to harbor a school. Where were the girls? Where were the nuns? What had become of that Renée who caused his exile to the hayloft? Of Claude he was certain. Claude could be read on any newsstand, once a week. Claude could be found. Claude had distinguished himself. At the turn of a telephone dial Claude's voice could be recovered: what a whirling veil of ancient dust! France was Egypt: the principle of Principal Brill's eclipse from the stars. Claude had called him Dreyfus. Claude, a critic of painting, drawing, sculpture: it was natural, predestined. The door opened; a small young nun put out her face, stiffly framed by a white coif. The back of Brill's shirt grew suddenly damp. "Hello?" he called. "I was kept here. Sheltered. This place hid me. I was preserved," he called. "A Jew. During the war." The small nun dipped her white crescent and smiled up diffidently, fearfully, from below it; she shut the door. Crazy people are known to be attracted to convents. Which war? She looked no older than a child of twelve. The four nuns who had ordered his salvation had doubtless been sent wherever it is retired nuns are sent: aged, severe, fatigued, themselves by now far from history; silent; dead. Yet Paris continued. Paris went on, not needing him. It was, he noticed, a lovely day. Through a slit of alley he saw, on the thronged avenue beyond, the summer tourists idling, fluttering their guidebooks and maps, fettered by their slung shoulder bags. He was a tourist himself, transfixed before this obscure city convent only in order to study the ferocious angels on the iron gate. It was no more possible for him to enter now than it would have been possible, having entered, to resume the dark life of the subcellar.

He went instead to the Musée Carnavalet. The courtyard was not as he remembered it: it was a thousand times punier and barer and grayer and stonier. His boyhood mind, submerged, flew upward, crowded with floweriness—explosions of concupiscence, petals so voluptuous they split of their own lushness, leaves glistering with such a density of greenness that they resembled, in his child's reverie, the flanks of slow-moving lizards. But there were only a few pots with sparse stalks stuck in them. Inside, he fled through corridors in pursuit of the sculpture of Rachel. Either it was no longer in its old place or he did not know how to find it. He asked the doorkeeper to show him the way to Madame de Sévigné's apartment, and was turned at last to her portrait—plump, clever, modern. The wind of fifty years, more than fifty, rushed at his head: it was as if he must hurry, this instant, to straighten the chairs for Rabbi Pult. The familiar anxiety over being late, a tightness at the neck. He was late, late; he would never again be on time. All the same it interested him that the Marquise was willing now to reveal only the thinnest lamina of her likeness to Hester Lilt, no more than a latency. A half-inch of chin, perhaps. Madame de Sévigné lacked the white wart. The rest—the lofty ironical aristocratic scrutinizing stiletto of her laughing look—was surely his own distrustful reading. His own shame. He was still dimly afraid of this place; his mother had made him afraid. It came to him then that he could retrieve Hester Lilt, if he wished, as readily as he could, if he wished, retrieve Claude. He could fish her up out of the telephone book; he could fish her up out of the belly of Paris. In this distant city (distant? why distant? aha, distant, he saw, from *school*) she was doubtless no more removed than his sister Berthe. The Musée Carnavalet had nothing for him; he left behind the courtyard that had made his child's heart shake with ecstasy and boarded still another bus. It wound around the Place des Vosges, with its eerie seventeenth-century restorations (only Madame de Sévigné could outlast time), through the roiling Marais, down the Rue des Rosiers. On this street, the street of his father's life, he spurned the window, his hands clutched the shoulders of the seat in front of him.

He thought he was headed for the sisters' flat, and he might have been; but he caught the brilliant crinkle of the Seine, the telltale leafiness that was the Tuileries, the honey-colored endless walls of the Louvre. It was still only early afternoon—impulsive as any other visitor, he jumped out and wandered among ancient dark paintings in baroque gilt frames. He understood how he was no longer a native of this place; he was no different from all these dozens of strangers, Germans, Spaniards, Danes, Italians; he sat on a bench and watched them come and go. Purposeless, he got up again, gravitating toward opening after opening, toiled up a vast stairway past bronzes and sarcophagi, and was startled, at the top, by the Winged Victory, mounted on a height of rubble. Headless, armless, an invisible sea-wind tossing her dress. The one eternal wing. He passed under the wing with a withered lung; it seemed to him he had entered here for Claude's sake, or for immortality's. He was lured on by the spoor of Claude, the perfumed cave under Claude's wing. He moved forward among churning bands of Englishwomen (schoolmistresses on a holiday: Brill knew a teacher when he spotted one, of whatever nationality), carried along by Englishwomen deeper into the classical galleries, past huntresses and gladiators, past a glowing torso of Apollo, past the powerful legs of a Spartan horseman. It was as if there had never been a Hebrew people, no Abraham or Joseph or Moses. Not a trace of holy Israel. In a modest recess near a door, massive, with the effulgence of a flood of white arrows, the Venus de Milo fell into view. The nipples of her breasts breathed. Her marble flesh was as luminous as though coated with milk.

Brill penetrated Mesopotamia, Assyria, Egypt: there sat an azure Isis on a throne of gold. He had a terror of these images and idols; Claude was drawing him, even now, into these rooms of beauty and light. A troop of adolescent girls marched by and he imagined that one of them, the last in line, whose pale hair, white-banded, hung down her straight spine and almost hid a tenderly pliant waist, was Beulah Lilt. In the incandescent twilight of this public cavern she appeared to him angelic, nearly as she had at Commencement, during the procession, only now the procession was going round the hall and gazing with vivid eyes at old Greek wine jugs. If the eyes were vivid, it could not be Beulah. Then he stretched his neck out again and saw that it was. Strange, to be dreaming Claude, the master of these resplendent forms, and to come instead upon this inert child, disguised in light! Once more she glided by him, eddying around the glass cases serried with painted urns. He called, "Beulah. Beulah Lilt." She turned, with her green stones, and took him in as if he had a flaw; she did not approach. He thought she must be too shy to break away from the others, so out of duty or civility he followed them into the next great lit chamber. "Beulah," he called. She did not look behind. The troop vanished into still another hall. Brill gave up and did not go after them. He lounged his way into the fine weather and found the right bus and went back to his sisters' flat and brewed another cup of tea.

From the bedroom Anne croaked: "Joseph? You're back?"

"I'm bringing the tea," he said.

She was sitting up, haggard and alert. "You've been seeing the sights?"

He told her he had been to the Louvre.

"It's very nice, isn't it. I should get over there and find out for myself what it's all about. Joseph," she said, sipping from a steaming spoon, "haven't things turned out well for you!"

"You all used to accuse me of drifting."

"You shouldn't hold a grudge, that was so long ago. Albert's a fine little chap, and now you'll have one of your own. Thank God you're married, Joseph, that's the main thing."

"Now you sound like Berthe."

"I should hope not. Iris says those renovations have brought everything up to date. She says you have the most up-to-date kitchen and bathroom."

"America's good at plumbing."

This made her laugh, and laughing made her cough. She held her breasts and he waited for her to subside. It was all at once as plain as air that she would not let him speak of long ago; she would not let him speak of loss. It struck him that he had returned to Egypt only to count his losses. Whereas his sisters counted blessings: the wisdom of old women. The ABCs were optimists and hedonists. They resisted memory. It was plumbing they meant to think about; they were like Iris. They communicated with Iris through Berthe, who had learned to speak English from her first husband, in the Manchester bakery.

"You're an important chap now, Joseph, n'est-ce pas? Iris says you have the biggest enrollment in the middle of America."

"Oh, she likes to blow things up," he said.

"She says the lake is beautiful."

"In the summer. In the winter it can get rough. The waves slam like earthquakes."

They talked on. Claire bustled back with Albert, the two of them giggling because they had not been able to exchange a word all day. "At my age I can't get my tongue started up on something new, and Albert won't even *try* to put out a syllable of French. But it's all right, he understood the trick riders, and Lord knows he understands croissants!" Albert had a whole bag of them, and a blue balloon from the circus; even the Rex had been a particular success, with, of all wonders, a Disney feature. Albert was chewing away on, Claire said, his fifth bun. Then Berthe and Iris came piling through the door, heaped with boxes both square and round: "I couldn't control myself, Joseph, I picked out *three* pairs of shoes, it was such a good price! Berthe knows the owner!" Berthe supervised Albert's washing up, and Claire set out the supper; Anne hobbled out of bed and sat at the table with the rest of them, wrapped in a winter shawl in July. Albert told about the clown who stood on one leg on top of another clown who stood on one leg on top of a horse, while a pink umbrella stuck straight up from the horse's jumping rump, and Iris said Berthe had shown her some really decent stores, the sort of places you'd almost expect to see back home, and Claire and Anne and Berthe argued about whether the potatoes were or weren't fully baked. Claire said they weren't; Anne said they were, she had remembered to put them in herself, even though a bit late in the day, because of falling asleep from her cold; Berthe said they shouldn't have served potatoes in the first place, done or not, they ought to have thought of something more festive—in a few days Joseph and Iris and Albert would be gone. Berthe said the trouble was that they should all have come to her for supper, then she would show these Americans what French cuisine was all about! And in a fine cherrywood dining room in a nice neighborhood! Anne said that was impossible, her head was a pillow of phlegm, she was on the verge of pneumonia, and all on account of Claire's pushing her into a boat that splashed, when anyhow it would have been more interesting for Albert to play with a new toy boat on the pond in the Tuileries. The Tuileries, *that* was seeing Paris!

This reminded Anne: "Joseph was in the Louvre today."

Iris said, "Isn't that the big museum they have over here?"

Berthe said, "It's famous all over the world."

Claire said authoritatively, "It has a Venus de Milo in it."

Albert said, "I want another croissant."

All the sisters gaped; they beamed. He had pronounced "croissant" perfectly.

"Iris," Berthe crowed, "if you leave your Albert with us for just two weeks more, we'll send you home a little Frenchman!"

Brill, pressing his knife-blade through a mainly raw potato, was not certain now whether he had seen Beulah Lilt after all. Schoolgirls of fourteen—she would soon be fourteen—often have pale hair, white bands, long wrists, scanty waists. If Beulah had stopped for him, what could he have said? How is your mother, Beulah? How are you getting on in Paris? Beulah, he might have said, what a grief you are in the world, to have fallen short of the heights! It's nothing to be a pretty thing like that at your age, but to be what you are, dry and plain, without a will, without a fire, flat, flat, flat, what good is it, defeat after defeat, nothing behind, nothing ahead, never to accomplish, never to distinguish yourself, to be the ordinary article while your mother's brain burns and burns!

He looked across the joyful table.

He was in deadly fear of Albert.

On the plane going home Iris went to the lavatory; she said she was bleeding in the strangest way. Brill shook with secret hope. A miscarriage would mark the end of his fear. "Look," she said, "if this one's lost, we'll get another. We'll try it again." "No," he said, "if this one's lost, we'll just let it go. I'm too old to be anyone's father." "No you're not, Joseph! You're Albert's." "All right then. In that case Albert's enough. One Albert's enough, it doesn't have to be by blood." He watched her redden. "I think you *do* care about blood. If blood's the thing," she said, "and suppose we've lost *this* one, then you don't want to stop too soon, do you?" These words, so familiar, so terrible, amazed him; they belonged to the philosopher, yet here they were, streaming out of his frivolous little wife. She had a new sweater of Brittany wool, a new bracelet hung with charms, a new tinkling necklace, each a present from one of the sisters. "You've done *very* well, Joseph," the sisters said when they kissed him goodbye. From an expensive English bookshop around the corner from her flat, Berthe had bought Albert a storybook to read on the plane; Brill did not tell her that storybooks bored Albert.

It was not a miscarriage, after all—only an unusual episode, and harmless, thank God—and in the middle of December the baby was born, altogether healthy. It was the son Brill hoped for. They named him Naphtali, after Brill's father. The day of the circumcision it snowed, not densely, but enough to sharpen Brill's excitement with a transparent film of ardor, like a lens that intensely clarified. Heaps of cheeses and cakes covered tables and dressers; the odor of smoked fish pricked. The guests stamped their shoes on the doormat, shaking off crystals—already they were melting into brilliant teardrops and leaving dark circlets on the mat. The child yelped like a torn sapling and was lulled when a cottonball drenched in wine touched his little tongue. Brill felt his own heart had been circumcised; he had cast off the natural skin of his old sad lethargy for this sacral lightness; he was a man like other men.

Albert was by now three months into the second grade; as if out of the air, Brill knew that there were other measures for life. All at once he stopped counting by the school year; he saw everything whole, everything was simultaneous! The infant, with its miraculous head, incited him to mystical emotions. Nevertheless he became normal. He explained this to Iris; but she laughed. "Normal people don't *think* about feeling normal," she said reasonably. Then she asked him whether the teachers were telling him anything about Albert: "Is he all right? Is he catching on?" Albert never liked to begin his homework; it bothered Iris; sometimes she shouted at him. Whenever Iris scolded Albert, Brill found work to do in his office; he had no appetite to enter those bright rooms over the playground, with so much furniture in them—the renovations were done with; it was a handsome apartment now. Albert had his own television set; he ate cookies in front of it, and played it very loud when he was supposed to be doing his homework. The baby cried in high huge swells whenever Iris shouted at Albert. Albert no longer liked baseball; he was too fat. Now and then Brill passed through the graveled bus lot and looked up at his own windows—it sounded almost like the Papageorgious' house.

But he was normal. It made the time go differently. He wheeled the baby up to the road, and showed him the rabbits and the blades of grass in the wind. Iris promised Albert he could push Naphtali on the swings when he was old enough. But Albert took to running away after school; he did not run far, only to the beach, jumping heavily from rock to rock. Some of the rocks were slippery, coated with a slimy moss. Iris worried about the danger, and made Brill go down to fetch him back for homework. "Albert, come up," Brill called, and looked out at the waves, wave after wave, and always the same wave. This meditation no longer scared him. All his old torments were dim. "Albert, come up!" he yelled. All the while he was thinking of Naphtali. He never noticed how the eighth grade vanished and returned, dissolved and reappeared. He became indifferent to Commencement and its lake-eclipsing sun-bruised dusks. The old cold cosmic knowledge of recurrence and perpetuity abandoned him; all the while he was thinking of Naphtali. Everything about Naphtali sailed on in a forward line—he always progressed, and he was always singular. You could not duplicate him—he was very bright. He chattered, his eyes sparked like Iris's; but he could learn anything, and in a flash. At four-and-a-half he was quicker than Albert at eleven; they put him right into first grade. At eleven he was quicker than Albert at eighteen. At eighteen Albert went from the Academy to a little Canadian college where they would make him into some sort of businessman; but what he really cared about was cars. He did not care about Naphtali; he said the only reason he was going away to college was because he was going away from Naphtali. At college Albert never asked for money; he seemed to have a whole lot of money; he never spoke of classes. Iris flew northward to account for so much wealth. Albert had a job in a garage in Hamilton. Iris came home laughing. "A trick like that!" she said.

But Naphtali was very bright. Brill thought about Naphtali's brightness all the time, not so much out of relief (though at first, and for a long time afterward, it *was* relief—Naphtali wasn't Albert) as out of bliss. When he remembered it—sometimes he *did* remember it—he resented that Hester Lilt had seen his terror. His terror had become his triumph. Anyhow he had never been afraid at all—she had attributed fear to him because of Beulah. But Naphtali wasn't Albert, Naphtali wasn't Beulah! He reckoned it out that Beulah must nowadays be a woman in her twenties. There was nothing to imagine about her but how old she had become now that she was fallen into the anonymous flow of humankind. He understood that he had never seen Beulah in Paris; in the Louvre it was only a wraith; it was wishful, he was thinking of her mother. Her mother did not belong to the anonymous flow, and yet Paris had swallowed her up all the same; he never heard of Hester Lilt. Her fame (she *had* no fame) was terribly narrow; one would have to be a reader of a certain kind, and he was not. It was only because her shadow had once been flung across his television set that he knew her at all. He had noticed her being noticed; that was her value to him. He recollected how the epistemologists had paid her homage: he supposed she was for the specialists, and always had been. In truth he had never been able to follow all her meaning. But she had thrown over his school a moment of high prestige—eight years out of more than forty *was* only a moment; he had tried to make the most of it; there was never again anyone like her; he admitted to having been dazzled. In spite of all that she was under an enchantment. She wasn't only a thinker, she was a woman. And what had her womb brought forth but Beulah! Iris with her plain brain was better than that! *Ad astra!* From the earth to the stars. Iris had gone, not without his combination, from the clay of Albert to the starry stuff of Naphtali.

Naphtali was the quickest child in his grade. His hand was always the first to shoot up. It was true the teachers deferred to him a little, because he was Principal Brill's son—still, they had begun that way with Albert too, until Brill told them not to. "Don't treat him any special way; don't treat him as if you think he's my son; he's not my son, you know," and then they treated Albert as he deserved. They treated Naphtali as he deserved, only with just a touch of deference—this time Brill did not object, because deference was just what Naphtali deserved. It was hard to tell what Naphtali was good at; he was good at everything; he didn't have a special talent, unless you counted pleasing teachers. He always asked for extra homework and extra projects, to please the teachers; but Brill knew it did not please them: it only made them groan, it added to their work, and Brill felt a private glee, because they didn't dare protest—who would be bold enough to meddle with Principal Brill's bright-eyed son? If the class had to write a two-page book report, Naphtali carried in a scroll; he told the whole plot. If the homework was to trace a map, Naphtali built mountain ranges out of plaster, and swiped Iris's pocket mirrors for the lakes. He was ambitious beyond anything; he wanted to go high. No one ever told him to go high; it was the way he was designed. "Give him his head," Brill admonished the teachers, "let him go full steam!" Only Rabbi Sheskin once said (by now he was married and the father of four tiny daughters—he had stopped looking like a camel-lidded boy; but his voice was still furry and sweet): "Naphtali, you should think about a sonnet, how spare it is. You should think about much-in-little. You should think about a phrase in Gemara, how concise. You should think about the smaller melodies of Mozart when young. You should think about the veins in a leaf." This made Brill angry. "Don't set limits on my boy! Concentrate on who you are! A little teacher in a little school! Don't judge my boy by your own size! You can't tie him down to your horizon!" Rabbi Sheskin said, "I was telling him about how a sonnet has only fourteen lines. Principal Brill, even for Shakespeare a sonnet has only fourteen lines, and I was telling him about Mozart—" "Never mind," Brill said, "stick to third-grade business!"

Iris brought Albert's television set out into the living room. Albert never came home at all. He had a partnership in a gas station attached to a used-car lot in Hamilton; his partner was a very good mechanic; Albert was living with a local girl, a waitress. Brill was relieved. Now there was only Naphtali.

After dinner they looked at different programs. They had to keep the volume down, not because of Naphtali's homework— Naphtali did his homework in a flash—but because of Naphtali's extra sixth-grade projects. This year both Seelenhohl and Gorchak were teaching sixth grade; Seelenhohl was teaching the American Revolution. Naphtali liked Mrs. Seelenhohl very much, as much as he liked Mr. Gorchak, and he was top in Gorchak's class. This softened Brill toward Seelenhohl. He began to think that perhaps class participation was a good thing after all—Naphtali did so well at it: Brill marveled at how quick Naphtali was at finding opinions to hold. For his extra Social Studies project Naphtali had the idea of compiling an Illustrated Biographical Scrapbook—it would contain the life-story, from birth to death, of every person who ever had anything to do with the American Revolution, whether on the British or on the Colonial side. He was working on it in his bedroom. His dresser was heaped with pictures cut out of half a hundred magazines. He meant to include Lafayette and any number of Hessians as well. It was his most ambitious project so far; it was so ambitious he had to consult often with Mrs. Seelenhohl.

"You don't want to do an *encyclopedia*, do you, Naphtali?" she chided him, and regretted it afterward.

Dear Mrs. Seelenhohl [Brill wrote]:

It has come to my attention that you have been discouraging Naphtali from pursuing a rather remarkable voyage into independent learning. If he produces prodigiously, at his young age, so be it, and I would hope his teachers would not find that an occasion for mockery. (As we all know, the Englishman Dr. Samuel Johnson wrote his own Dictionary, and my own countryman Diderot produced exactly that which you mock: an Encyclopedia!) Please be good enough to help Naphtali all you can with the gathering of sources. He especially needs more reproductions of well-known portraits. Perhaps you could spend some time in the library with him (the town library, if ours proves deficient) after school hours. I wish I could offer some monetary recompense for this, but you know our budgetary dilemmas.

Faithfully,
J. Brill
Principal

It was not Brill's habit to confide his school deliberations to his wife, but because this letter was about Naphtali he came out of the kitchen—he had written it straight off on the kitchen table—into the living room to show it to her. She was sitting in front of the television set, rattling her bracelets in a way that annoyed him. He had only lately grown conscious of the different things she did that annoyed him. She read the letter and shut off the set. "Oh Joseph," she said, "I don't know. They get paid little enough for their regular time—" "Now look. Don't start making financial policy. You don't know *what* they get paid. You haven't been near the books for a dozen years. They get paid more now than they got paid then." She reflected a moment; she was a month past forty, and there were scalloped lines hidden under her bangs. "You know what I think of this letter, Joseph? I think it's an old man's letter. That's what it is." "You don't know what you're talking about," he said, keeping back his temper. "Seelenhohl hasn't done a stitch of real work in years. It will do her good to put in a little time—I'll enjoy seeing that. She's a sloth. She's a sluggard." "Naphtali likes her." "Naphtali likes all his teachers. Naphtali likes school. Naphtali likes learning." "That's only because he likes coming out on top," Iris said. "Would you rather," Brill flashed, "have him run a gas station?" "You used to be more of an idealist, Joseph. You used to care about fairness." "Now I'm a father, so I care more about ambition." "Whose ambition?" she said smartly. "Naphtali's." "Only an old man would say a thing like that. You don't want anything for yourself any more. Not even me."

It was perfectly true. He *was* an old man—he was nearly seventy-six, and in spite of the reminders of the Administration Committee he was not thinking of retiring—and she was the most trivial woman on earth. Nothing she said interested him. She referred often to his age; she referred to it as if it was becoming a derision between them—not the old playfulness, but something new and grave and mean. Her voice was loud. She had too much loose hilarity, she was too bustling, and all her bustle went into making herself glitter. She dyed her hair tarry black; it was a river of gleaming pitch; she had always dyed it to catch the light. She oiled her elbows and her nose and the scalloped lines on her forehead. She poured golden ropes around her neck and over her wrists. She owned a hundred rings. He calculated how, with a little more education, she would be just like Seelenhohl; with a little more than that, just like Dr. Glypost; with a little more (and minus her golden chains), just like those epistemologists long ago. She did not prevent him from putting the letter in Seelenhohl's box.

He sat with her every night and they looked at television—but always very selectively, and with the volume turned low, so as not to disturb Naphtali in his room. They looked at all the good things on Public Broadcasting: famous old movies, bits of ballet, interviews with museum curators, and once a whole opera. Brill mainly dozed in his chair. "That's what old men do!" Iris hissed. The rich benefactress had died years ago; her son and two daughters were running the Administration Committee. Two of Brill's sisters had also died: Anne and Berthe. Claire had moved into Berthe's flat; she was now the owner of the cherrywood dining room. She had turned stone deaf. He grieved more for his father and mother, for Gabriel and Loup, for Michelle and Louise, for Ruth and Rabbi Pult, than for the sisters. He was used to grieving for his first losses; it was as if he could not bear the extra weight of more. Naphtali was now the only one on the planet dear to him. The ABCs had never met Naphtali, and in their letters had often neglected to ask after him; but they remembered Albert well and heartily, and for Albert's wedding (he married the waitress in Hamilton, Ontario) Berthe sent him half a dozen huge tins of croissants from the finest *pâtisserie*, elegantly wrapped in gold-leafed paper, as an affectionate allusion to his Paris appetite. Most of the croissants arrived broken; heaps of crumbs. Such a foolish woman. Despite Iris's taunt he was not asleep, but not attentive either; he heard the name Lilt—did he hear it? or was it another false lure, still another crumb of Paris, or else a remnant of nap he had fallen into after all?—and jumped into alertness. "What's this?" "Something about Europe again," Iris said, "they're always showing foreign stuff on this channel." "Is it Hester Lilt?" "It's about art." "No it's not," Brill barked, "she's got nothing to do with that. Make the thing louder, can't you?" "Naphtali's working," she chided him.

He leaned forward and turned up the volume. Background music ballooned—something modern-sounding, distorted and high-pitched, like wails—and then letters, words, voiceless, rolling downward, a waterfall. He read on the face of the tube: NEW MOVEMENTS ABROAD—THE ART FRONTIER. "Did you hear Lilt?"

"*I* don't know, Joseph, you're going to annoy Naphtali." He said impatiently, "She used to be one of our parents." "Who?" "Hester Lilt, I told you." "You've never mentioned anyone like that." "It was long ago. She left. She went away."

The letters and words rolled out of sight and two people, a bald interviewer in glasses that enlarged his eyes enormously, and a woman wearing a shirt and tie, slid into view.

"That one's too young for a school parent," Iris said.

The man and the woman had begun to talk. Brill stared. "That's not Hester Lilt."

"I didn't know you were so crazy about modern art, Joseph."

"Be quiet," he said.

Naphtali called from his room, "Hey in there! I can't hear myself think!"

Iris dutifully moved a knob. The voices receded. The interviewer was asking faint questions and the woman was faintly replying. It was a program about new young painters—a new school. They called themselves Caryatids—was it, the interviewer wittily put it, because even dream should have a base in theory? The woman undertook an explanation of the new theories; it was difficult to follow. A work of art, she said, was like the water inside the hump of a camel: a life-sustaining liquor that could not be seen except through the shape it conferred, and could never be known except through its effect on the rider. It was a form without a discernible presence. She conceded it was uncommon for a school of painting to be led by a theorist, but tonight they would meet her on camera—she had already had several exhibits in Paris, her work was making its way in London, and one of her shows would shortly be going to the States, to the Guggenheim Museum in New York, in fact. After that, Chicago and Cleveland.

"Boring," Iris murmured. "Bor-*ing*."

A third head appeared. Brill saw at once that it was Beulah Lilt. She instantly contradicted the interviewer and the woman wearing the tie: she was not a "theorist," she did not believe in "movements," she was nobody's leader, and she certainly did not ride camels. There was no movement and it had no name; it was only that she had called a series of her own paintings Caryatids; everything else the newspapers had invented.

"Oh Joseph, for heaven's sake."

"You were educated in the States," the interviewer was saying.

"I don't think you could exactly call it an education." (Audience laughter.)

"Is that a comment on the absence of camels in America or on the present state of painting on the Continent?" (Audience laughter.) "Still, you went to primary school in the Middle West?"

"I think I did. At least my mother says I did." Beulah's voice! High and utterly clear; clarified. She no longer sounded American. Her hair was cut short and held by two butterfly pins. Brill again calculated her age: twenty-seven, twenty-eight, twenty-five. It struck him that her eyes seemed stupendously lit. Contact lenses? The studio lights? Who had polished those green stones?

The interviewer pursued, "Don't you know for a fact anything about your schooling in the States?"

"I can't remember it."

"But if your mother says—"

"My mother lies a lot." (Audience laughter.) "It's her occupation." (Audience laughter.)

"What occupation would that be?"

"Mother." (Audience laughter.)

"Surely," the interviewer pressed, "the mother of Beulah Lilt has got to be different from other mothers. As a matter of record, she happens to be Hester Lilt of L'Institut Philosophique—"

"That only means she writes down her lies." (Audience laughter.)

"Good God, who cares?" Iris said. "Joseph," she accused, "what's the matter with you, you don't like this stuff any more than I do."

The inside layers of Brill's nostrils were burning; he felt he could not breathe, it was impossible he was really hearing all this. Not a word about Dual Curriculum! As if it never existed! As if it

never was! As if nothing, nothing! It was a hallucination, a mirage;
once again he was flying after a face that was no face, a voice that
was no voice. A wraith.

The wraith faded off, but the program was not over. The woman
in the shirt and tie explained that the next guest would be the art
critic of L'Empressement, the distinguished Paris weekly. By now,
blow after blow, in the necromancy of his subterranean doze, Brill
knew what he would see before he saw: something like a djinn,
capable of any form. The critic's English was excellent, perhaps
even a shade more elastic than it had been at the time they crossed
the Channel together, but—unexpectedly—he had a wrinkled
wattle that made Brill think of an emptied-out testicle sac. His
drifting cheeks were no different; they hung like used vacant
balloons. He was too thin, much too thin, and his hair was thin,
though still vivid. Brill thought: he touches it up. How old and
spectral Claude had become! Surely it was Claude; blow upon
blow, phantom after phantom, Egypt devouring Osiris. Brill gave
an immense yawn; he inhaled fire like a furnace; Iris was right,
he had no interest in this stuff, it was more comfortable just to
yawn and doze. Still, he ordered himself to attend. The woman
in the shirt and tie, sober and respectful, was asking the djinn—
this old, ruined, wrinkled Claude—incomprehensible questions.
Claude said he agreed with Mme. Lilt's judgment on herself, she
had been quite to the point, she was indeed no theorist, but all
the same she had set the Paris galleries on their ears. Why is that,
the interviewer inquired, sober and respectful. A type of latency,
Claude replied, in a British English so pure that Brill was compelled
to acknowledge how aristocracy is aristocracy, no matter what: it
can command the subtlest noises of the world; it listens to the
very birds. "The latency," Claude peeped (with a certain birdlike
emphasis, sharp and bright), "of Idea; she has," he concluded,
"an indisputable subject."

Was it Beulah, was it Claude? Decidedly it was Claude, though
desiccated. His translucent eyelids folded of their own accord, like

peeling Chinese screens. Therefore it could not have been Beulah—
what did Beulah have to do with Claude? Claude who had required
him to learn a whole stretch of Pierre Louÿs in a translation
Joseph could barely pronounce? And if it was Beulah—he was
sure it had been Beulah; he was certain, at least, of *that*—then
how could it have been Claude, Claude in all his boy's beauty
long ago?

Nevertheless Brill waited. He watched the announcements,
scouring unfamiliar columns in journals he scarcely recognized.
He waited for Chicago or for Cleveland. Somehow he missed one
city, so it was to the other he went; he took Naphtali with him.
Iris complained of the cost of a hotel room overnight, and for no
sensible purpose, not to mention his wearing Naphtali out with
such a long drive just before exams; but Brill told her it was
important to give the boy a taste of something different, what else
was an education all about?

"In that case," Iris said, "you might as well take him to the
Guggenheim directly! You might as well drag him all the way to
New York just before all his tests!" "It's time he saw New York,"
Brill said. "And Paris? Next thing you'll say it's time he saw your
sister Claire! *There's* an education—she can send him cookies for
a wedding present!"

Brill did not answer; often he did not answer his wife. What he
wanted was a witness. He led Naphtali up a slanting ramp and
looked through phantasmagorical windows enclosed in narrow
silver frames. The corner of each dense yet gossamer window was
signed Beulah Lilt. It was true, it was true. "What do you think?"
he asked his son; he noticed how Naphtali's eyes grew startled,
with a kind of click, and how his tongue slipped in and out.
Naphtali would oblige him: he would say whatever it was right for
him to say. Brill tried to imagine what was right. It wasn't that all
these curious windows were "abstract"; it might be that they weren't
abstract enough. You could fancy amazing scenes in them: but
when you approached, it was only paint, bleak here, brilliant

here, in shapes sometimes nearly stately, sometimes like gyres. The purity of babble inconceivable in the vale of interpretation. That old dewlapped bag-of-bones scarcely knew his own business: she had no "indisputable subject." Once, from four feet away, he thought he was gazing into a scarlet ditch, from hip to heel, in the haunch of a nude female: the ditch was crowded with two double-rows of fat human toes with coarse yellow nails. It unnerved him—but when he came near he saw it was again only paint. There was no nude, no ditch, no horrifying meat-red stuffing of live toes. "Is this artist famous?" Naphtali wanted to know. Brill brought him back to the hotel then; how early in the evening he felt his fatigue!

Naphtali, too, was tired, but going to bed in a new city he had never before visited excited him. He asked the desk clerk for a map and in the lobby picked up a handful of brochures on local sites of consequence. Within an hour, bending over hotel station-ery with a hotel ballpoint, he had mastered Indian burial grounds, pioneer history, founding fathers, the location of City Hall and the Rotary Club, as well as which minerals characterized the neighborhood; he could also tell the price of every movie in town, who the neurological specialists were, which Presidents had passed through, the names of luminaries (including a celebrated opera star) who had been born either in the central city itself or in smaller towns nearby. There were clues in the telephone book, on a wall chart over the toilet, and even on an old ticket someone had left in the Gideon Bible, right in the middle of Job. Naphtali's lists were ingenious; he loved categories, divisions, classifications, types; he loved orderliness. But Brill was distracted. "They have a trolley museum!" Naphtali called out from the bathroom, where he had found still another historical hint. "They have a monu-ment to Napoleon!" "Napoleon?" Brill said; "here?" "Anything's possible anywhere," Naphtali said in his elderly way.

The purity of babble inconceivable in the vale of interpretation. Brill thought to himself: *In the morning sow thy seed, and in*

*the evening withhold not thy hand: for thou knowest not which one
shall prosper, whether this seed or that. . . .*

Pult: *At forty Akiva had not yet begun to learn, and still did
not know anything. Once he was standing by a well in Lydda and
said: "Who made the hollow in that stone? And who polished this
stone?" They answered him: "Don't you know, Akiva, what is
written in Job? 'The waters wear away the stones.' "*

The sin of withholding his hand.

Who had polished those green stones?

When they came home, Iris asked, "Well? Was it worth the
trip?"

And bright Naphtali cried, "Look at all my lists!"

Meanwhile, treachery: Seelenhohl lodged
a complaint against Principal Brill with the Administration
Committee; Brill's last letter was put in evidence. He was becoming more and more unreasonable. He was too old, he was unfit.
To demand a teacher's free time for private tutoring, and for his
own son! Was he accountable to the Committee or was he not?
Was this selfish tyrannical preposterous old autocrat supposed to
be a school principal or was he not? The Committee hesitated. It
argued with itself. Remember, the rich benefactress's son said,
where he came from, what happened to him in the war. You can't
just shove out someone like that. On the other hand, the rich
benefactress's daughters said, were they to be in thrall forever to
his past? He was all right now, wasn't he? Was he never to be
removed because he had once gone through a bad time, and so
long ago? Was he to be a perpetual exception from the laws of
ordinary need? Was his history to become an idol, and the school

its shrine? Didn't the good of the school count for anything? Were they to be tethered to an old man always, out of pity?

The Committee—gently, cautiously—requested Brill to choose his successor. They wrangled with him for weeks and months; they waylaid him and they wheedled; he understood he was beaten; anyhow he was tired. The rich benefactress's son, a certified public accountant, with uncharacteristic passion suggested Rabbi Sheskin. Sheskin as Principal! "Rubbish," Brill spat out. "He discourages ambition in the bright ones. He nearly squelched Naphtali. He lets the dullards languish, he lets them do anything." As a special courtesy his own vote was given extra weight: he voted for Gorchak. Gorchak was fair. He respected the Dual Curriculum and its founder. Principal Brill's retirement was set for the following winter, almost half a year away—the Committee, piously honoring the late benefactress, agreed there was no great hurry— but Brill was uneasy. Gorchak all at once appeared to be giving orders without consulting Principal Brill, the true head and founder. Brill saw that Gorchak knew how to make the Committee laugh; he did not shrink from saying the most impertinent things right *at* them. He told them they should behave as their mother would expect them to behave, as if all of them (the sisters in their fifties, the brother in his sixties) were a pack of children. He could make the eighth grade laugh out of shame, the seventh, the sixth, the third, and now even the Committee.

M y God, Joseph," Iris called one morning in the spring, near the end of his tenure, "isn't this the same girl from that museum show you dragged Naphtali to? She's all over the place, and here she is again." He thought how painful it was to get out of bed so early; it was the hiring season. A long day of interviewing lay ahead of him. He looked at the magazine Iris was showing him. She was always showing him magazines with Beulah Lilt's picture in them. He read: PAINTER OF THE YEAR. Miraculous. The face seemed too dense, more like a heavy statue than a photograph, why was that? The eyes were green stones splendidly polished. He did not understand how this had come about, this illumination. She was older; different; each time he encountered Beulah Lilt's face it was more puzzling, harder to recall. She did not resemble Hester Lilt.

From his bed he telephoned Gorchak. Gorchak was delighted to take on the job of interviewing; after all, he knew what made a good teacher. Someone lively, with a sense of humor and drive; someone who can tell an industrious pupil from a lazy one; someone herself very bright. What he would look for was a history of high marks; he would skim the cream. It went without saying that he would have to use Principal Brill's big dark office and sit at Principal Brill's impressive desk in Principal Brill's Bristol chair, with its hand and globe: otherwise he would fail to show authority, and how could he hire successfully without a show of authority?

Sitting in the Bristol chair at Brill's desk in Brill's office, Gorchak was struck by a handsome young woman, brown-haired, with a mouth somewhat puny, a nose somewhat broad. She was recently married and would undoubtedly soon be pregnant. But Gorchak was not a bigot like Principal Brill, he intended to be progressive, it was clear to him that a healthy woman could teach well into the ninth month; in any case, you couldn't defy the new laws on these matters. Besides, Gorchak knew this young woman's record even before looking into her dossier. The interview was a reunion, an embrace. She had been one of his own best pupils.

Brill, frowning over the list of newly engaged teachers, saw a red check near one name.

"What's this?"

"My prize," Gorchak announced. "A find. She just walked in the door, out of the blue."

"Mrs. R. G. Korngelb."

"I regard her as very able. She won the Hebrew Composition Award at graduation her year. What a class that was! You remember Corinna Luchs?"

"Corinna Luchs," Brill said dully.

"Our highest-ranking valedictorian. The finest record we've ever had. She made it into Harvard right out of the Academy."

"Luchs," Brill said. The leader of the pack. The pack flying after; Beulah Lilt, the tail. "Bright child. Excellent essays. Fine insights. Harvard."

"She's vice-president in charge of public relations at one of the airlines now. The youngest they've ever had. She writes all their brochures. Her mother keeps in touch."

"You mean *you* keep in touch, Ephraim. You're on top of everything. You'll be good for the school. You'll be in control."

Gorchak scratched at the list with a gratified forefinger. "Mrs. R. G. Korngelb! Imagine, it's Becky! Rebecca Gould, she used to run with Corinna."

"I remember that."

"I've put her high up, Joseph. Right into the seventh grade. Social Studies. A sociology major but she can handle history."

"Mrs. Seelenhohl won't like that. Not someone she taught." He distrusted Seelenhohl. She had proved herself treacherous; he wanted to keep out of her way. "Put her in fifth."

"Mrs. Seelenhohl?"

"Mrs. Korngelb. We've never had a case like this before," he said doubtfully. "One of our own."

"One of our own, exactly! She knows our values here. She knows what we want because she's lived up to it herself. A coup, Joseph," Gorchak said; he had never before dared to utter anything but Principal Brill. "In a year or two she'll be ready for eighth. Anyhow we should think of retiring Seelenhohl. She's always been a lazy cow."

"Ephraim," Brill said carefully, "from that same class, do you remember Beulah Lilt?"

"How could I forget? If you'll permit me, Joseph—one of your mistakes. She should never have been admitted in the first place. She couldn't handle it. Bottom of the class. The mother was divorced, or a widow, anyhow no husband, quiet like the daughter I think, never showed up in school, never did anything in the P.T.A.—"

This dependable fool now called him Joseph! "The mother made a little name for herself. You never noticed that."

"That children's book?—no, it couldn't be. Wasn't that Mrs. Lillian Lebow, the one who did the dancing alphabet?" He blazed out a rosy square-toothed grin under his finely-cut nose. "What do you think of my day's catch? The return of the native, a success story!"

Brill said, "Yes. A success."

"She never got less than one hundred percent on any of my weekly tests."

"Ephraim, don't brag. The fact is we grow pygmies here. Did you ever give a thought to that? A republic apart. They never marry, they never bear fruit. Fair-faced and beardless into eternity."

"Oh, not true, Joseph. They all marry."

"I worry for Naphtali. I'm too old, I won't know what becomes of him—"

"He'll be Principal! I'd better look out!" Gorchak joked.

Gorchak joked; he joked as he would with a child, because Principal Brill was old, and the old are like children. Gorchak had his little family, the boy and the girl, the worried little wife; when he stood, he cast a shadow like other men. Brill admonished himself: Gorchak exists; Gorchak sees me, and I see Gorchak; we cast our two shadows; Gorchak is not transparent; it is necessary to have serious feelings about Gorchak. But he did not know how.

Watchfully, watchfully, Brill took note of Beulah Lilt. She was too intricate for him. For a while he was vigilant and rapt, but after a time he admitted to himself that one had, in a way, not to be so tired, or to specialize in all this, or to be interested at least in current movements; in art history; in visions. He discovered he was interested mainly in Naphtali's schoolwork.

The Committee—always gently, cautiously—was attempting to force him out of the hayloft. "After all," the certified public accountant said, "it *is* for the use of the Principal. That's in the contract. I didn't remember that myself, but my sisters did." In over forty years no one had ever spoken to him of his contract; they were boors. "Joseph should be Principal Emeritus, shouldn't he?" Iris howled; she was furious at all of them, the whole Committee. "Haven't we lived here for years and years? And Joseph *founded* Dual Curriculum, only now you want to forget that! My God, this school wouldn't have a *name* if not for Joseph!" "Suppose we leave," Brill said; he had never relinquished his loathing for the hayloft. "Anyhow Naphtali will be ready for the Academy before we turn around." Naphtali was already fluent in French; Naphtali's French was first-rate. Brill himself had begun to sit with Naphtali in the evenings, listening to irregular verbs. Naphtali loved the permutations of verb tenses; he loved to conjugate. It irritated Iris when Brill and Naphtali recited together in these peculiar syllables; it reminded her again of Berthe's wedding present to Albert. "Why don't you just leave the French teacher something to do?" Iris asked.

Secretly Brill thought Naphtali should go to a more distinguished high school than the Academy. Naphtali should go to the Sorbonne. You couldn't get into the Sorbonne from the Academy;

it didn't matter that Corinna Luchs had made it into Harvard. The Sorbonne was the Sorbonne. "You know what?" he said to Iris; he was being very mild. "Maybe Naphtali ought to go over to Paris for a while. He could polish up his French, and it wouldn't be too expensive—he could stay with Claire, and try out a term at the Sorbonne, to see if he likes it."

"With Claire!" Iris said.

"She's all alone, it would do her good."

"And what about Naphtali? Would it do *him* good? She can't even hear the doorbell or the telephone. He'd end up being her butler. He'd spend his life shopping for groceries in all those stupid little stores. He'd end up being her maid. He'd end up running a nursing home."

He had no answer for this; she had lately grown fond of cruel truths. It was so: the handwriting in Claire's letters was fading, turning fainter and fainter; it was as if the pen were a weighty oar she barely had the strength to pull.

"Well, we might do something else," he conceded.

"What?"

He was dreaming. She would tell him he was dreaming like an old man.

Brill said, "We could think about retiring to Paris."

"Paris!" she yelped. "Rotten stores and dinky kitchens. My God, I'll never forget your sisters' bathroom, and after all the modernization we've put in *here*? Paris once in a lifetime's enough."

Naphtali protested, "I don't want to be an astronomer anyhow."

"It isn't just astronomy. I did that," Brill explained, "but you can study anything you want to at the Sorbonne."

"Well, why *not* astronomy?" Iris said.

"It's not the road to the stars."

This made her laugh. "What *do* you want to be?"

For some reason they had never before asked Naphtali such a question; he was too protean.

"A teacher."

"Oh, a teacher!" Again she laughed her loose laugh. "Don't you get enough of them around here?"

"I want to give homework," Naphtali said.

Brill could no longer follow Beulah Lilt's track; he could not keep up with her. It was not only that she was too much a swimmer in a sea he could not penetrate or fathom—a lethargy had settled over him. It was like the lethargy of earlier years, but then he had contradicted it by running; now he walked under an evil spell. Arthritis compelled him to go with a cane. Iris, meanwhile, was subject to migraines; whenever she felt one coming on she flew up to Hamilton to visit Albert and his wife and their new baby. When Iris was gone Brill would often enough find Beulah intimately revealed on television, her head and eyes and bright teeth large and close. Or it would seem to be Beulah, himself in a doze before the glimmering casement. He understood she was acclaimed. He understood more: the forms, the colors, the glow, the defined darkness, above all the forms of things—all these were thought to be a kind of language. She spoke. The world took her for an astonishment. She was the daughter of her mother. "Your Paris painter," Iris threw out from time to time, "just look, another prize for something, since you care—" She handed him a clipping. He read it and got rid of it. He felt embittered by her language; he could assimilate it even less than her mother's. The light and the dark, the colors, the transmogrification of forms: strange violent quick tongues, she could talk!

He never again, not even in a reverie, saw wily old evanescent Claude, with his translucent lids and joggling wattle.

Brill drove with Iris to a slide exhibit at the university, in the same auditorium where Hester Lilt had lectured on Theory of Pedagogy. Naphtali had his eighth-grade project for Gorchak, and refused to go. Iris too was truculent. Beulah Lilt's paintings, one after the other, announced by a clean click in the cave of a dimmed chamber; and then a film of Beulah talking, in that captivating way that caused hilarity. All around them there was

laughter. Brill was embittered, bewildered. Iris said, "Boring, how
can you stand it? I'll never sit through such a thing again. Don't
ever try to make me. What's this obsession, this dragging everywhere? You never *used* to make such a fuss about art," in the tone
he knew; it meant she was betrayed a thousand times over.

In the end they had to vacate the hayloft. Brill was relieved.
Anxious little Mrs. Gorchak was installed in Iris's up-to-date kitchen
with all its specially built cabinets. Gorchak reigned over Brill's
office; but Brill had taken away the Bristol chair and the portraits
of Freud, Einstein, Spinoza. The *Ta'anit* he left behind. Fleg's
Beast he threw out. Everything in the capacious drawers of his
desk he threw out, one geological stratum after another. It was a
long afternoon's work; he stopped to look at whatever he found.
Packets of old letters from Claire: "Drifter." And from Berthe: "Be
fruitful and multiply, Joseph! 'It is not good that the man should
be alone.' Marry, Joseph, take a wife!" The letters were decades
old, and in their inmost creases he caught the tiny movements of
whitish larvae. Under a weight of third-grade compositions (why
were they there at all?—then he remembered: Fifferling had dumped
them before leaving) Hester Lilt's paper, still in the envelope marked
BY HAND. Fifteen years ago Iris had collected it from Beulah; it
looked just the same. He took in the bright blue ink of BY HAND
and reflected how Iris had ravished him on that same day, the
saucy tongue, the saucy bangs, the enchantment! A new fright
stirred in his teeth. Sorcery. How the wormlet mockery swells to
become the strangling serpent. He had obeyed his sister Berthe—
late, late!—and redeemed his life. The gates of Eden: they were
going to verdant Florida, with its hot winds, to be near Naphtali.
From the back of one of the drawers he pulled out a forgotten pair
of socks, crusted with dried mud. Naphtali's—they had green
stripes across the top. The apple of his eye. Naphtali had done
well at the Academy; he always did well, but he had his own ideas.
Iris said, "He has his own ideas." They never spoke of Naphtali's
polishing his French, or of the Sorbonne. Iris would not allow it.

Iris said, "He's better off without that place." Brill raised Hester Lilt's envelope to his nose, as if moths might announce themselves with a hot smell, like Florida.

For the first time he read what she had written all the way through. He saw that finally it was not about Structure or Silence at all. It was long, demanding, allusive, obscure, pain-giving, tedious; he had to put on the lamp. An old, old voice. He no longer needed to pay attention to it. The last section was called "Schoolmistresses" and appeared to be simpler than the rest. It was about the pelican and the stork. He recognized the stork: it belonged to Rabbi Pult. She had pilfered one of Brill's own tellings.

> The mother pelican [she told] with her fish-catching bill in the form of a pouch that distends: her white-headed babies dip into it to pluck out the little fish she keeps for them there. Ah, what a good mother! Ideal parent! In folklore the pelican in her piety is thought to feed her young with her own blood. You can see them suck out her heart.
>
> The Jews call the stork *hasidah*, which means lovingkindness. The stork, though her beak is slender and straight, is the pelican's cousin and shares her fame. She too loves her little ones; profound is her love for her child. Yet the *hasidah* is deemed impure. The hen and the duck are kosher, the goose may be eaten; the stork is forbidden. Such a doting bird, conscientious parent, model to the indifferent duck and hen, the inferior goose! But she loves only her own. She hopes only for the distinction of the little one under her heart. She will not cherish the stranger's young.

Aesopian woman! The fox, the bee, the cannibal galaxies, Akiva laughing! Thief of Pult! Brill crushed her words back into the envelope marked BY HAND, and by hand flung it after Naphtali's socks, Fifferling's compositions, his sisters' ancient complaints, Fleg's *Beast*. Beasts and beasts, her didactic bestiary, her heraldry, her filchings, her accusations, her daughter, her daughter!

In Florida they took a modest house in a neighborhood of refined retired people who frequented the public library, walked abroad carrying Russian novels and plastic bottles of milk, attended lectures, read the *New York Times* a day late, and said their subdued "Good morning" from behind flowering hedges. Iris pointed out that it was all really very like a respectable district in Paris. Naphtali was now a sophomore at Miami University, majoring in business administration. He lived in the dormitory and came home every weekend. Then, little by little, he came less and less often. "He's getting used to all the racket they make down there," Iris said. "It won't hurt his grades," Brill said in his new fatigued way; it seemed to him he sounded frightened. "No," she agreed, "it won't." Naphtali had changed his mind about becoming a teacher; he thought of empires. He thought he would found companies, induce them to accrete, and then forcibly amalgamate them: he would work day and night, grow very rich, and be tapped by the President for, say, Secretary of Transportation. He would resuscitate cross-country land mobility, commanding untried alliances among buses and trains; he would air out the crackling grease of the bus-stop cafeterias that lay across the breast of the nation; he would wash the windows of the dozing trains; in the cities he would plant twin silver tracks in black urban asphalt, and bring streetcars to life again. How pleased the President would be!

Occasionally Gorchak would send down a friendly letter in which he would explain every change that he had made, all of them urgently needed—the question of the name of the school, for instance. It was now called the Lakeside Grade School.

It's really in homage to you, Joseph, that I have seen fit to recommend this fresh appellation [Gorchak wrote]. The Edmond

Fleg Primary School has been ineradicably associated with you, with your origins, your temperament, your experience, your own elucidations, and, if I may say so, your own striking tone, or accent, in daily speech. All this has, it goes without saying, bestowed charm and glamour upon this institution, and it was appropriate, during your tenure, for the Francophilic atmosphere to be maintained.

We are, however, on the brink of a new generation, for whom the European capitals have little, if any, meaning. The European experience is irrelevant to our new generation, even, or especially, among our young parents. It would be less than candid of me if I failed to note that the literary allusion in "Edmond Fleg" is opaque, however pregnant and meaningful it has been to you all these years. Many parents have not understood it. It would be (I know you will agree) a bad risk for such an important institution as ours to continue under a name so little comprehended by the public we hope to reach and serve. Loyal to the name though we all have been, surely you have also been aware of it as a handicap in fundraising. My hope is to increase enrollment by as much as one-third, and contributions by considerably more than that, and under the truly picturesque and sylvan name "Lakeside," so reflective of our watery surroundings, I have every confidence that we can accomplish this fine goal. The members of the Committee, I must confess in all modesty, are with me all the way in this significant matter.

Indeed, we all continue to miss your "Tale of Two Tantes," but surely you, Joseph, would be the first to utter "Ad Astra" for the Lakeside Grade School! (By the way, we have also removed, as you will have observed, the colophon "Ad Astra" from our school letter-head. All this is part of my intent to streamline and modernize. I know I have your sympathy in this effort. But at your own generous instigation we are retaining "Ad Astra" among our dearest memories in a most indelible way, as you will see in the enclosed.)

Gorchak had tucked in a copy of the latest P.T.A. Bulletin, compiled by Mrs. Sheila Frucht, a fifth-grade mother well known, Gorchak noted, for her fine writing talent:

Mrs. Rebecca Gould Korngelb, one of our school's most distinguished alumnae, mother of three, and the eighth grade's most
lively and popular teacher, not to mention her being an attractive
brunette in her own right, now moves to the other side of the Dual
Curriculum as well; she is the first teacher in our school's history
to teach on both sides of the Dual. What a brain! In addition to
Social Studies, she will take over Principal Ephraim Gorchak's
Bible History class. Principal Gorchak has his hands full just running
the school! Congratulations on super achievement, Mrs. Korngelb!

Mrs. Seelenhohl announces her retirement after many years of
beloved service. Happy rest-time, Mrs. Seelenhohl!

The Administration Committee announces a $100 prize, to
be called the Joseph Brill Ad Astra Award, and to be given at
Commencement to the eighth grader with the most creative potential regardless of class standing. This unusual category was chosen
by our sorely missed ex-Principal himself.

Rabbi Sheskin regretfully ceases his employment here, following
his star no doubt to greener fields in another school where we hope
he will be as appreciated as he has certainly been with us. Shalom
and better luck elsewhere, Rabbi Sheskin!

Brill's chin rested on his chest. He was afraid he would never
have the power to raise it. It was age; it was something else. Even
in Florida, curled in the Bristol chair, his hand on the hand that
held the globe, he dressed in wool. He was old and cold. He had
a tall young wife still; everyone remarked on it; this much was the
same. But there was something else. Sometimes he remembered
what it was. Sometimes he almost remembered; usually he forgot.

Whenever he happened on Beulah Lilt—if he read about her,
if he stumbled on her photograph, or on photographs of her
paintings, if he saw her head lift on the screen like a sculptured
apparition, or if he imagined her as his dream's incubus, or if he
conjured her by will, with open eyes, or even if he found her in
his mind through some accident of searching—he was amazed.
He was amazed! Not that she was "original"; he was by now used
to that. Not that she was acclaimed; this seemed as natural as air.

Not even that she could talk. But he succumbed to the iron belief (when he remembered it) that her mother had spoiled his life— had, in fact, waylaid him, plundered and robbed him. In hindsight he knew he had been ambushed by Hester Lilt.

He heard nothing ever again about the life and work of Hester Lilt.

But Beulah Lilt's language assailed him endlessly, endlessly. It oppressed him. She had forgotten her childhood in the Curriculum that was his treasure and his name, as dear to him as his son Naphtali. She labored without brooding in calculated and enameled forms out of which a flaming nimbus sometimes spread.

A NOTE ON THE TYPE

The text of this book was set in Electra, a type face
designed by William Addison Dwiggins (1880–1956)
for the Mergenthaler Linotype Company and first made
available in 1935. Electra cannot be classified as either
"modern" or "old style." It is not based on any historical
model, and hence does not echo any particular period or
style of type design. It avoids the extreme contrast between
thick and thin elements that marks most modern faces, and
it is without eccentricities that catch the eye and interfere with
reading. In general, Electra is a simple, readable type face
that attempts to give a feeling of fluidity, power, and speed.

Composed by Centennial Graphics, Inc.,
Ephrata, Pennsylvania
Printed and bound by R. R. Donnelley & Sons, Co.,
Harrisonburg, Virginia

Designed by Judith Henry